Vickie Johnstone  lives in London, where she writes on magazines and edits books.
Some day she hopes to live by the sea with some
fluffy cats and a lifetime supply of Milky Bar chocolate.
Her children's book, *Kiwi and the Serpent of the Isle*,
was a finalist in the Indie Excellence Awards 2013.

By Vickie Johnstone

3 Heads & a Tail

Cerulean Songs
The Sea Inside (book 1)

I Dream of Zombies
I Dream of Zombies (book 1)
Haven (book 2)

The Kiwi Series
Kiwi in Cat City (book 1)
Kiwi and the Missing Magic (book 2)
Kiwi and the Living Nightmare (book 3)
Kiwi and the Serpent of the Isle (book 4)
Kiwi in the Realm of Ra (book 5)
Kiwi's Christmas Tail (book 6)

Smarts & Dewdrop Series
Day of the Living Pizza (book 1)
Day of the Pesky Shadow (book 2)

Poetry
Kaleidoscope
Life's Rhythms
Travelling Light

Others
The Gage Project charity anthology
Published by Inknbeans Press
(Contains some of my stories and poems)

The Sea Inside

Cerulean Songs, book 1

Time is all we have;
it flows – it cannot stop

By Vickie Johnstone

The Sea Inside
Copyright © Vickie Johnstone 2013
Published by Vickie Johnstone, May 2013
Written between 2009 and 2013

All rights reserved

No part of this publication may be reproduced, stored in a retrieval system or transmitted in any form or by any means without the prior permission in writing of the publisher, Vickie Johnstone, nor be otherwise circulated in any form of binding or cover other than that in which it is published

Printed and bound by CreateSpace

ISBN-13: 978-1490417547 (CreateSpace assigned)
ISBN-10: 1490417540

Acknowledgements

Special thanks to Maja Drazic for her wonderfully expressive photograph that adorns the cover of this book.
www.maay.deviantart.com

Thank you to my beta readers, Greta Burroughs, Nicole Storey and Jennifer Thomas, for offering to read my first draft and giving me the confidence to publish it.

Dedicated to all the dreamers.

Part One

Jayne concentrated on getting better. The dark mood that she had found herself in grew steadily lighter and she pushed her memories of the blue city to the back of her mind, dismissing them as dreams, which would gradually fade with time.

That was her hope, for while she slept her mind wove images of the sea, accompanied by the echo of the whales and a tall man whose hair was the colour of the darkest waves.
He was always there, not far away it seemed, thus was the lucidity of her sleeping life.

Chapter 1

Jayne awoke in a cold sweat, her T-shirt plastered to her chest and stomach. A hazy impression of the dream lingered in her mind; water and something blue sparkling in sunlight. She remembered shooting pains in the soles of her feet as if daggers pierced the skin from myriad directions. Jayne blinked and used her arms to raise herself up into a sitting position. The room was beginning to brighten as light struggled to flow through the dark, heavy curtains.

It must be morning already, she thought, rubbing her eyes, but the ward was too dim and quiet. The two patients at the other end of the room were asleep, as was her friend, Charlotte, who lay in the bed opposite. Careful not to wake anyone, Jayne reached across the blanket for her book, which lay downturned in the very spot where she had left it before dozing off, and she quickly located the last line she had read. Upon turning the page, something shifted along the edge of her line of vision and a shadow cut across the floor. Startled, Jayne glanced all around as an ice-cold trickle crept over the surface of her skin. The ward was still silent and no footsteps sounded, yet the shadow swept closer. The book dropped from her hands.

"I didn't scare you, did I?" asked a face, which seemed to appear out of nowhere at the foot of the bed. It wore a thin smile.

"Well, yes, actually you did,' said Jayne, reaching for her book. She drew it protectively against her chest.

"Who are you? The nurse..."

"I'm sorry. I didn't mean to scare you," said the woman, who looked to be about sixty years of age. She was wearing a long, dark blue coat and matching hat. "I wanted to speak to you before anyone else woke up. I visited before, but you were not awake then."

Jayne surveyed the ward again. None of the patients had stirred, but then the lady had walked all the way to her bed without appearing to make any sound at all. The air, so still, made her nervous. The older woman continued to smile, the grin etched deep in the folds of skin around her mouth. Lines creased her eyes, which glinted with an energy that made them seem years younger than the rest of her face.

"Perhaps I should call someone?" Jayne asked timidly.

"There is no need. I only wish to speak to you. Please don't be afraid of me. My name is Sophia Ambry. I read about your accident in the newspaper. It was such a sad story. The reporter said you were a gifted runner before..."

"Yes," Jayne replied with a sharp grimace. "I was, but I can't talk about it." She felt odd for saying anything at all, but there was something about the stranger that made her want to speak, despite the edginess she felt.

"I understand," stated the woman, opening the dark, woollen bag she carried. It was beautifully embroidered with blue shapes of various sizes.

Jayne relented, leaning back against the headboard, wondering whether to press the alarm button by her bed. She shivered for no reason and then told herself there was really nothing to worry about; the woman was obviously harmless, but clearly eccentric, and perhaps lonely.

"I want you to have this," said Sophia, smiling awkwardly. She pressed a small, black velvet bag on to the bed next to Jayne's hand. "It is a dear thing. Another one rescued me when I, too, felt very alone and it brought me back from where I had been sleepwalking. Use it wisely. Once gone, it is gone forever."

Raising her eyebrows, Jayne stared down at the bag in surprise.

"Don't be frightened, please. I bring you a gift. Please take care of it. I am too old to need these things anymore. Remember that time is all we have and it never stops," breathed Sophia.

To Jayne's horror, the old woman then stroked the back of her right hand, which lay limp on top of the bed cover. Her wrinkled fingers were like ice. The young girl's eyes raced up to the old lady's face, but she was already gone, simply vanishing into the air, as if she had never been there at all.

Jayne surveyed the ward, but a hush cloaked everything. No one moved, no shadows played, and the stranger was nowhere to be seen. She rubbed her eyes, wondering if she had blacked out again for a while. It often happened nowadays if she became anxious. Shuffling under her blanket, Jayne leaned carefully over the side, drew in a breath and peered under the bed, but there was nothing on the floor. She frowned. Light was beginning to stream through the curtains and she expected everyone to wake up soon. Where was the nurse?

In that moment, Jayne spied the small, velvet-looking black bag, sitting in the folds of the blanket. A black cord secured the top. She stared at it for quite a time before deciding to pick it up. It held secure in a knot. Curious, Jayne tugged it open to be greeted by a familiar smell, reminding her of blissful holidays spent on the beach when she was a child and her parents were still alive. "Wet sand and the sea," she muttered to herself.

Whatever was inside was weightless for the bag did not weigh a thing. Jayne swallowed. "Don't be scared, silly," she whispered to herself. "She was just a harmless old woman."

As she tipped the velvet, an odd-shaped piece of glass tumbled out and glinted in the ray of sunlight peeking through a crack in the curtain. On closer inspection, she found it to be a fine, small crystal of shimmering blue and quite beautiful.

"Morning, sleepyhead," Charlotte called out from across the room. She had just woken up and was offering her usual friendly smile.

Jayne pushed the crystal back into the soft bag and shoved it under her pillow. "Hey, sleepyhead yourself," she replied, but her cheerful response sounded shaky. She still carried the stranger's enigmatic smile and perplexing words in her mind.

Chapter 2

Every night Jayne experienced a recurring dream in which she was running across an empty beach, her red hair blazing in the sunlight, sweeping, flying in the wind. Dancing and twisting in the sand, her feet sank into the cold, damp heaviness. She charged forward with Glen barking in the breeze, leaping over him as he spun around, his tail wagging for all it was worth. The midday sun beat down on them from a clear blue sky dotted with silken wisps of softest white cloud.

But it was only a dream.

Jayne would never run along a beach again and feel the coolness of the water trickling between her toes. She would be able to smell the sea, its salty breath, but never feel it against her legs. She would never run, never walk; never sink her feet into the soft sand. Wincing at the thought, Jayne fought back her tears. She stared down at the two bumps at the bottom of the bed, which lay motionless under the blanket, imagining them as two stiff branches stretching away. They did not feel heavy. In fact, she could not feel them at all. They seemed no longer a part of her as she felt no sensation in her body from the waist downwards. She gritted her teeth and stared up at the white-painted ceiling and its whirring fan.

Maybe this will not be forever. Everyone is so hopeful, so perhaps it won't always be so, but how long do I have to wait?

Jayne felt like she had been lying in the same bed for an eternity. She yearned to run and feel the sensation of it, just to feel anything, but she was stuck here in this ward and had been for six weeks. The doctors said she was not fit to go home. Her body was still fighting the infections and numerous issues that accompanied her injury. With a start, she realised that she had lost track of time. Earlier, she had been sleeping, trapped like Sleeping Beauty in a quiet coma for three weeks. Upon waking, she had been disorientated and ill for a time, but it was nothing compared to the shock of being told that the lower region of her body was paralysed. Her legs no longer worked or else they did not want to.

The doctors had their theories, and her friends and relatives had a million more. Jayne had one: she was not meant to walk any more. Yet, deep down, part of her still held on to the belief that she would. Perhaps one day her legs would just start working; just decide, 'You're going to feel us today, and wake up, and get up, and step out of bed to do all the simple things that you once took for granted'.

Her dearest friend, Michael, had hope. He believed the coma had been her body's way of healing itself. He was always so cheerful – well, most of the time – so perhaps she could manage to smile today when he visited, or at least not bring his mood down yet again with her endless pessimism, and think of all the stories of people who did walk again. Even if she didn't, her life was not over; many people who had survived accidents like hers learned to adapt and lead rich lives. She was only sixteen after all. She had her whole life ahead of her.

Yes, a whole life in bed! No!

Jayne gritted her teeth and shelved the bad thoughts to the back of her head. Today was going to be a good day. She would smile through physiotherapy and imagine her legs working, and be positive. That was what her grandfather kept telling her: try to look on the bright side, even when things seem their darkest. He had brought her books on the power of positive thought, and told her stories of people who had been in comas for fifteen years and woken up, or people who... well, just numerous miracles really because they still happened each and every day.

"Hey, how's Miss Happy today?"

Jayne glanced up to see Michael striding towards her bed. "Fancy coming for a spin in my car later on today?" he asked.

"Yeah, sure, I've just got to get showered and dressed first," Jayne answered with a wink.

Michael always cheered her up. They had been friends from the age of eight ever since she stopped the biggest bully in the class from pushing Michael around, just by telling him he smelled, making the rest of the children laugh. Jayne smiled at the recollection. She felt so happy when he visited her; his infectious grin was like the sun on a rainy day. Not that life on the ward was so bad. The food was good, all of the staff seemed nice and it was the best hospital for rehabilitation, if that was the word, and there had been many success stories here. She just had to keep on hoping. Hope was everything.

Chapter 3

It was summer, Jayne's favourite time of year, and the sun streamed through the windows as if to remind her. She was gathering strength in her arms every day; everyone noticed. Her wheelchair was becoming easier to use and she was starting to play sports in the hospital facilities, although she was still slow and uncoordinated. The doctors wanted her to go into the pool as it would help, but Jayne winced at the thought and the black nightmares would surface. She could not bear to think of all the water, not even once.

It had been weird to discover that her photograph had been in all of the newspapers months earlier. There she was, in black and white, staring back; a pretty, smiling sixteen-year-old girl, holding a trophy for winning a race. Alongside it was another image of her, but lying in a bed with tubes everywhere. The owner of the swimming pool was being sued and his picture was there as well. He looked stressed, but it was not really his fault, Jayne knew. It was an accident; a really bad one, but still an accident.

All her friends had been splashing around in the pool at the time, taking it in turns to dive off the highest board, Jayne remembered. She'd had a feeling it was too challenging, but did not want to be the one who chickened out. While she had never attempted such a height before, it looked straightforward and she had conquered the board below. The technique would be the same, she assumed. As she weighed the options, her friend, Angela, smiled and waved encouragingly as she climbed out of the pool, dripping wet.

So up Jayne had gone. She ascended the thin ladder and stepped out on to the board. In that split second when she gazed down, she sensed it was wrong; it was all so wrong. Something didn't fit and she should not jump, but the instinct in her body seemed stronger. It was almost as if she knew something bad was about to happen, but she could not stop herself. It was too high and then it was too late; she had taken the dive and she was crashing down towards the water.

Below, Jayne did not hear anything as her head made impact with something solid and then came the pain, sharp and unforgiving. She struggled to get back to the surface, but the right-hand side of her body would not work and she was unable to stand. Then came the darkness, soft and still, offering an escape that cloaked her like death.

Then there was nothing at all until Jayne woke up disorientated and unable to move her head, surrounded by the familiar faces of her grandfather, Angela and Michael. For some reason she could not fathom, they were all weeping as well as smiling. At the time Jayne had not known they were crying with happiness because they had been afraid she would never wake. A machine beside her made funny noises and there was a tube in her hand, and then Jayne realised she was not at home; she was in a hospital and her neck was in a brace.

Although she felt weak, she was happy to see her grandfather and friends, even though her body was not doing what she wanted it to do. While Jayne could raise her fingers, they were stiff, and her arms felt heavy and awkward. Her right side was also much weaker than the left and there seemed to be very limited movement, but most frightening of all, she had no sensation in her body below the waist. She tried to move her legs and found she could not. There was no feeling in them; nothing at all. The realisation made her feel helpless, lost and alone.

Later came all the explanations from the doctors and her neurosurgeon. Jayne was told that her upper body felt stiff due to her having lain motionless in a coma; her muscles had literally gone to sleep. When she hit her head in the pool, what they called the cerebral cortex had been injured, leaving her comatose for nearly three weeks. She was told there might be lasting damage to any of her senses, the way she perceived things or more complex thoughts. The information only confused her as it sounded so vague.

Besides the brain trauma, X-rays had shown Jayne's neck to be broken. The impact in the pool had caused the bones in her spinal column to crash into one another, shattering the C-6, the sixth vertebra down, leaving only movement in her arms and above. While Jayne's upper right side was also partially paralysed, the break in her neck had not completely severed the spinal cord nerves, leaving a window of hope.

The neurosurgeon performed an operation to remove the fragments of bone pressing on Jayne's spinal cord, leaving a three-inch scar in the hollow of her neck. The shattered bone was replaced and secured with a titanium plate. The belief was that her vertebra would fuse with the implanted bone.

Unable to remember much about the accident, apart from the searing pain and a feeling of everything closing in, Jayne asked her grandfather what had happened. He informed her that the lifeguard at the pool had rescued her and performed chest compressions, and an ambulance had been called. All her friends had gathered around in shock, according to Angela, who had accompanied Jayne to the hospital. To everyone's horror, she did not wake and the coma lasted three weeks. At the time, Jayne's grandfather had been informed that if it had lasted longer than four months, the probability of her making a full recovery would have been very low. Feeling helpless, he had wished he could switch positions with his granddaughter. It made her upset to hear him say it.

Recovery was the word Jayne was most interested in. While the doctors found it easy to explain her injuries, they appeared less confident about the probability of her body healing itself completely. That was a question to which no one had an answer, simply because spinal injuries were so unpredictable. Time will tell, they kept saying, as the weeks of therapy flowed into one another.

Leaning back against the headboard, Jayne shook her head and blinked away her tears. There was no point in thinking about all of that again. It was too painful. The best thing was to try to forget it and look forward; to think of something brighter, even when everything seemed so dark.

Chapter 4

The white-painted corridor loomed ahead of her, unremarkable in its familiarity. *How many times have I come this way now?* Jayne had lost count. Here and there, chips and dents interrupted the smooth, even surface of the paintwork. A bit like life, she thought, stopping the wheelchair and folding her hands in her lap.

It was one of those endless days. Michael was on holiday and had been gone for four days so far. The place seemed silent without his loud company, and Jayne was not expecting anyone else, which made it a hard day. Her grandfather had a cold, so he was unable to come, and everyone else was clearly far too busy. Even Charlotte was away, on a home visit.

Ah, but that's selfish, Jayne admonished herself. *I shouldn't think only of myself; must not keep thinking in this way; not linger on depressing thoughts. It's pointless. Everyone has their own life to lead. They always make an effort when they can. I should feel lucky for that.*

Biting her lip, Jayne lifted her head to gaze out of the window. David, the guy who never spoke, was sitting in the garden staring at the trees while Jessica fed the birds. A shiny blackbird with the brightest yellow beak perched in the branches staring down, almost daring her to move away, so he could swoop and land his prey or a piece of bread in this case. Feeling her mood lift slightly at the sight, Jayne wheeled her chair towards the door, which opened as she approached, allowing her to go outside. *It really is a beautiful day. I should not take this for granted. I could so easily not be here, not have made it out of the pool...*

Jayne blinked. The sun sat low in the clear sky and she had to squint to look in its direction, but it was welcoming. The birds chirruped low and comforting. Jessica had moved to talk to David. She was one of the few to whom he opened up, but he had been in the hospital a long time. In the tree the blackbird still lingered, dipping a tail feather and bobbing his head. Jayne looked up and he seemed to stare back at her, making her smile. If only he were not so timid; if only he was brave enough to fly down and sit on her hand as if it were a perch. Then she could feed him and stroke him; make contact.

"If you trusted me, we could just sit here looking at each other," Jayne whispered. She imagined the softness of the bird's feathers and the chill of his tiny feet in her hand. "But, aren't you warm-blooded?" she asked. "Wouldn't your feet be warm?" The little blackbird chirped and bobbed again.

When the air grew slightly chillier, Jayne went back inside the ward to continue reading her book. She tried to ignore how the day dragged, the minutes ever stretching: lunch, physio, dinner, her book, the garden, nothing on television, bath, back to the book and then sleep, the realm of imagination. That was the best time for in her dreams she was running on the beach again and it was blissful, the sea lapping against the soft sand, making patterns as the white surf blew bubbles. Neither clouds nor pain existed, just freedom, her body whirling in the breeze beneath the glorious summer sun.

Jayne woke, hot and covered in sweat, feeling as if

she had not slept at all, but her clock said 3 a.m., meaning that she had been out for six hours. Hugging herself, she remembered the dream, so perfect. It was too bittersweet to wake like this. *If only Michael was here.* She could talk to him and he would understand. He always had something funny to say that made her laugh. A single tear trickled down her face and she wiped it away, but it was followed by one more and yet another. Before she knew it she was crying. *I must not think like this; I must think forwards.* She bit her lip so as not to make a noise and wake the other patients.

Reaching into her bedside cabinet, Jayne pulled out her bag. Women's secret places, her grandfather called them. "I wouldn't dare go into one of those," he always said. She half-giggled at the memory, spluttering through her tears, and pulled out a tissue. "I must not cry. It's silly," she told herself. "I won't be here forever, because nothing is forever."

Jayne gritted her teeth and removed another tissue. As she did so, her hand dusted something extremely soft. Peering inside, she spotted a smaller, black bag sitting at the bottom. "I had forgotten about you," she said, grasping it.

So fine, seemingly fashioned out of the finest velvet, the bag must have been expensive. Pulling it out, Jayne wondered where the old lady had bought it, or whether she had made it herself. On closer examination the velvet was not so black after all, but a sort of midnight blue; the darkest imaginable. Or perhaps it was black and looked blue in the light? A bag of many colours, she surmised.

Remembering the beauty of the object inside, Jayne undid the string that secured the material. It was such an unusual present to give someone, especially a stranger. The orb of glass glinted. Although there was barely any light at all in the room, the crystal glistened; a myriad blues, all interwoven, and there was something at the centre. She placed the bag down on the bed and held the crystal up to her face. The blue seemed to swim. There was definitely something there at the heart of it, but it was too dim to see properly.

Curious, Jayne gazed closer, but the glass glinted again and the mist within faded. I'm so stupid, she chided herself. *Of course there is nothing inside.* She sniffed. No, she told herself, she couldn't keep crying. What she really needed was more sleep. It was just a bad day; that was all. Michael would be back soon and she could confide in him.

As another tear trickled down Jayne's face, she sighed and wiped it away. *This won't help anything.* Then another droplet fell, splashing on her hand and scattering across the surface of blue, which seemed to shimmer more brightly. Jayne blinked. The glass began to blaze with a stronger hue, showing a fervent mist swirling inside. Squinting, she gasped as the brightness blinded her for a second and then the crystal splintered, slicing into her palm. A burning sensation shot through her hand and feeling dizzy, she closed her eyes.

Chapter 5

A burning sensation in my hand forced me to open my eyes. I blinked in disbelief, closed them and reopened them once more, but the scene remained unchanged. The sun was shining, yet it was not yellow. Instead it was red; the exact shade of blood. This deep russet sun glowed in a sky of dark blue, bereft of cloud, blazing with an unusual brightness.

I raised my hand in front of my face to shield my eyes. A thin, bruised line trailed down the centre of my palm and I remembered. Where was the cut? I could have sworn the glass went deep. Checking my other hand, I found it held the crystal, still in one piece. Carefully, I placed the object in the pocket of my tracksuit bottoms and rubbing my eyes, I took in my surroundings.

I was lying on the ground and it was curiously warm, so I surmised that I must have wandered into the garden. Also, I remembered being in bed when I cut my hand, so perhaps I had fallen asleep and sleepwalked out here? But I had never done such a thing in my life. Unease washed over me. Raising my head and shoulders slowly, I leaned back on my hands to gaze up at the sky again. The sun was definitely red; that was not a mere figment of my imagination. It suddenly dawned on me that I was not in the hospital garden and I sat up with a start. I was in a forest.

A lush, green wealth of trees stretched way beyond the height that trees normally went. A carpet of red, green and golden leaves surrounded me, interspersed with tiny twigs. Up above I spied a break in the foliage through which the sun flashed down amid that strange, dark blue sky. Frowning, I gathered my thoughts. *Perhaps I had left the hospital garden, but why was the sun red and why was I in a forest, and surely I could not have got here alone?*

I wondered if I was actually dreaming still, but everything felt so real, and I was dressed in the same clothes that I had been wearing in the hospital bed: a black T-shirt and zipped purple-hooded top, black tracksuit bottoms, and a pair of pink, fluffy socks... no shoes. "Well, it isn't as if I'm going to run out of here," I joked to myself.

Instinctively, I glanced around, half expecting someone to have heard me. Then I recalled something else. My wheels must be here somewhere, I thought, looking around again, but not seeing my chair. *Perhaps my family brought me here for a picnic or something, and I had one of my blackouts and can't remember? Then again, maybe it is all some kind of joke?* The situation did not make any sense to me and the sun was definitely red.

"Michael?" I called out. "Is anyone there?"

The wind whistled through the trees, but no reply was forthcoming. I would just have to wait for someone to come along. Raising myself up further, I stretched forwards to smooth down my trousers, which were covered in leaves, and to my shock I felt a tingle in my knee. I gasped as my leg quivered. It was impossible. Yet there was also an itchy feeling from my thighs downwards. Spreading my hands over my knee caps, I was astonished to find that I could really feel them, truly. My breath almost stopped as I tried and succeeded to move my toes. Frightened, I stood slowly and somehow I did not collapse.

I laughed and the sound echoed. I spun around on my feet, which did what I willed them to do. It was the first time I had walked since... I stopped. *I must be dreaming still.* This was only a delusion, a fantasy, and that was so unfair. Soon I was going to wake up and all of this would be a product of my imagination.

"But it feels so real. How can I be thinking this up?" I asked aloud, but the forest had no answer for me. I pinched my arm and yelped, and then laughed at myself. "Well, that isn't proof. That can happen in a dream!"

Perhaps my injured brain was playing tricks on me. I had been in a coma after all. Stranger things happened every day. Who really knew what the mind was capable of? Turning, I took a step and felt a sharp stab in the underside of my right foot. "Ouch." Socks and no shoes did not a good scenario make. Checking my sole, I found nothing stuck there or on the ground, so I took another step. "Ah!" The same stinging sensation shot through. Every time I walked it hurt. Now I was sure of fantasising. It was like Hans Christian Andersen's tale of the little mermaid who was in discomfort when she walked. That decided it for me; I was definitely still asleep and dreaming. I sighed to myself. Obviously, I had been reading far too much.

As I trod forwards, I gathered my surroundings. Bereft of any breeze here, the sun felt hot, even though the forest was dense and the trees so tall that I could not see where they ended. The branches stretched up like fingers on all sides, reaching up to something beyond. Catching sight of a blue mist lurking in the distance, I thought of the haze inside the crystal - the exact same shade. It seemed my imagination had remembered it and placed it into this crazy reverie. Yet it was the most lucid mind trip I'd ever experienced in my life.

I spun around. The forest was soundless, save for the rustle of leaves beneath my toes, and I was definitely alone. "Which way should I go?" I asked aloud. The mist seemed thicker to my right and dispersing somewhat to my left, and I decided to follow it. The forest smelt green, yet the indigo colour appeared to strengthen. Even the leaves on the ground seemed to become bluer, but perhaps that was my fervent imagination too. After walking for half an hour or so, a growling in my stomach reminded me that I was hungry. I hoped my brain would conjure up some appetising food and quenching drink, and also some treacle pudding and custard, and...

A sharp crunch startled me. It came from behind, way back in the direction from whence I came. An icy trickle of fear crept up my back to the base of my neck and I quickened my pace. The misty trail through the trees made me think of fingers beckoning me forward. The closely packed trunks began to grow less dense and I noticed how their bark sparkled with iridescent streaks of blue. A low hum filled the air, but it disappeared if I listened too hard; it was almost as if the trees were breathing. I knocked the idea out of my head straight away as it was completely surreal. Well, almost as crazy as being in a dream that seemed to be real, and also one in which I appeared to be able to make choices.

Again, I heard a sharp crunch behind me, like breaking twigs. I began to run, surprised by my ability to do so, and I travelled into the cobalt mist that grew deeper in hue. For some reason it felt safe. I gradually broke into a sprint, checking carefully where I trod as I ran, certain I would fall at any second on my newly found feet. Somehow they did not take a wrong step and I charged on, my red hair rippling out behind me in the wind. Something was following, I knew it, but for some reason I did not feel afraid. Instead, I felt the opposite. I was running and I felt free.

Abruptly, the trees stopped, literally fusing together to create a living wall of impenetrable wood. Stretching out my fingers, I felt along the familiar roughness of bark, but these trunks were even bluer here. I stood still and listened into the void of silence. Behind me something was still coming. I sensed it, even though I neither saw nor heard a thing. To my right the mist lingered, and there looked to be a gap between the forest and the wall of trees, forming a kind of passageway, filled with light the colour of ultramarine. Without thinking, I chased down it, the leaves rustling in my wake.

On and on I ran into the blue. Gradually, the mist grew so thick that I doubted being able to find my way. I would have to trust my feet and hope I didn't crash into anything. Soon the way ahead darkened, but it was not black. No longer able to see my hands, I slowed down. A gloom stretched behind me, with a clear blue dot of light at the very end. I could not see anyone there, so I carried on walking ahead, tracing my fingertips along the bark to my left. For some reason I still did not feel frightened. I was caught up in the experience of walking; a simple thrill that left no space for fear. Onward I trod.

Weirdly, I began to detect movement along the forest floor; perhaps the leaves, I thought, but soon it felt as if the very ground was shifting. I pressed on, feeling the wall of protective trees with my hand, but soon I gave in to the blind urge to run again, hoping I would not stumble. Something pulled at my feet and it was not the little shards of pain that I was becoming accustomed to with every step. It was something else; something as cold as ice.

Picking up my pace, I ran into the dark. My heart pumped loudly as though trying to burst through my chest, and I was breathing so hard that I heard myself panting. I had to calm down somehow. Behind me echoed the crunching, but I dare not stop or turn in case the icy fingers entwined themselves around my feet. *What were they, and what would happen if they managed to grab a strong hold?*

I took a deep breath and sprinted faster. The line of bark turned sharply and I ran with it, and after a short distance it turned again. Weaving to and fro, it reminded me of a maze. Again it curved and then stopped. The forest ended without ceremony and I found myself looking upon an endless ocean.

Chapter 6

I stepped out of the greenery and on to sand. The icy fingers had abandoned my feet and there lay the sea, dazzling in its full, colossal glory, but gazing on it brought my fears to the fore. Up above shone the biggest moon I had ever seen; wide and white with silvery edges, looming so brightly in the darkness. Yet it was not really so; as before, this sky was of the deepest midnight blue, not black. All around me circled the familiar mist that had been my guide thus far. I could see clearly and it was deathly quiet. Only the waves dancing along the shoreline broke the hush that reigned.

I stepped along the sand, enjoying the sensation of my feet sinking into its soft depths, although I wished for something warmer than socks. It was colder here beside the sea and a strange wind howled out there. It fought against the silence and I was not sure if I could really hear it over the stillness, so deafening. I coughed, unable to hear myself, and then I saw the shadows. They were all around me, all at once, but then they were gone just as quickly.

Feeling hands grip my feet, I looked down, yet there was nothing to see. Fingers pulled at my hair, invisible to the naked eye. Bewildered, I felt unable to separate what was real from what could not possibly exist. Cold fingertips traced a line around my face, but I could see nothing. I screamed, but my voice was lost in the deafening silence. In front of me the ocean rippled, perhaps offering sanctuary, yet I dared not approach, for the water petrified me. My memories of the pressure and pain, the dark all-enveloping cloak of near death, were too fresh. In my mind I relived the feeling of being slowly suffocated all alone. "No," I breathed aloud, trying to suppress it.

I ran along the edge of the lapping water, screaming as an invisible entity charged behind me. I heard it dimly and then it was gone, lost in the unbearable quiet that seemed to suck up every sound in the air. *So my dream was turning into a nightmare, but what kind of torment was this?* My feet sank further into the sand, which thwarted my efforts to run faster. I knew I had to stop feeling such blind terror. If I panicked, I would fall.

In the blue dark I thought I heard a piercing wail, but then the hush. Perhaps it was my own terrified voice or maybe it came from the sea; I could not tell. I kept running as though I were racing some invisible competitor. In the past I had always managed to outrun my opponents and I hoped it would be so again. The eerie wails rose up again before dying as suddenly. Gradually, my sense of horror crept up on me and I began to feel so very frightened. I was completely isolated and my body was tiring. *How much further could I run?*

Ahead, I could not see where the sand ended. It appeared to go on and on forever, and the sea seemed as fathomless. *When will I wake?* I so wanted to wake. Turning my head, I peered over my shoulder as my red hair whipped my face. There was no one else on the beach and the forest was now a distant block of black, growing steadily more blurry. Something still chased me, even though there were no footsteps in the wide, empty expanse of sand; only my own imprints.

My breathing grew heavier. I needed to stop. My legs had almost given up anyway. Something was coming; this thing I could not see. It was inevitable, I knew. Now and then I thought I caught a shadow flickering at the edge of my vision, but then it slipped away. The air grew colder and I weaker. My hair cut across my eyes.

The ground gave way unexpectedly and I fell flat on the wet sand, one of my feet twisting into a shallow hole. I coughed, spitting out particles of sand, knowing I had to get up. It was coming. I could hear my heart pumping over the top of my own breathing and I steadied myself to stop gasping in panic, but I realised I would not be able to get up in time. Whatever was here was so much stronger, so much faster than me, and I had no more strength to run. My hair whipped in the wind and covered my face, and I left it there, no longer wanting to see what was coming for me.

Coughing again, I struggled to catch my breath and then a rumble of wails started up from the depths of the darkening sea, becoming increasingly higher in pitch. I covered my head with my hands. The ear-splitting sound exploded into the air, knocking the silence into the sand. I closed my eyes and waited for the end. Perhaps now I would wake. I read somewhere that you cannot die in your dreams.

The icy wind blew harder and I buried my face against the damp sand as it roared. In the distance the wailing grew louder as if the sea itself was crying. Something knocked me flat on my back. Freezing cold fingers flickered in my hair and fixed around my throat, squeezing. I screamed, unable to visualise my attacker, yelling ever louder until I was sure my lungs must burst as the hands covered my face. Kicking my feet, I fought back with my fists, but I could not feel anyone there. *Was it some kind of ghost?*

Chapter 7

Spluttering, I struggled against the insane desire to lose consciousness. In the midst of my panic I thought I saw a face with eyes the colour of the sea and hair to match its furthest depths. Then there was nothing but the roar of the waves and blackness even darker than the deepest blue. "Come into the waves," the voice said, piercing the silence and jolting me back to reality. As though waking, I tried to move my head, but something frosty kept it flat against the wet ground. I was lying on my stomach, tasting salt in my mouth, and I guessed my eyelashes were sprinkled with sand as they felt heavy when I blinked.

"Into the waves," repeated the voice, its tremors sailing softly upon the lapping water, roughly a metre from my face.

My legs twitched; something had a firm hold of my ankles. My heart raced and my voice caught in my throat. The thing in my hair was trying to force my face down into the sand, so I fought back, battling to turn my head away. My right hand was also trapped, but I could not feel it. A firm weight pressed down on that side. My fingers were sinking slowly into the sand, which seemed to be giving way somehow. I wriggled my neck around, yet I could see nothing in the darkness and it was growing so cold. The dark glowered.

I wondered how long I had been lying here, guessing that I must have blacked out in my panic, but why had I still not woken from this nightmare?

"Come into the waves before it is too late," a voice whispered and then the wailing began again, screeching and deafening, so loud as to be against my ears, and I fought to free my hands to cover them. My left hand, whose fingers now lay in the line of surf lapping at the shore, I could suddenly move, so I flicked my palm further out into the water, feeling a welcome strength return to it.

"You must come now!"

In the dim haze I was certain of seeing eyes – eyes in the sea; the face with dark hair. They stared back at me, bobbing on the waves, but nothing frightened me more than the water. I could not go in. Memories of the accident flashed through my head like a slow-motion reel. I slammed the images to the back of my mind and glanced down the length of my body. Invisible hands were still attempting to drag me downwards and I realised that I would eventually suffocate in the sand; a slow death. If there had been something real and tangible to see, it would not have scared me so much as this, but here there was only the feel of icy fingers and unseen claws, and this eerie wailing.

I had to face my deepest fear, but why was I so afraid? This was only a nightmare, I reminded myself, and nothing can harm you in your dreams. Stretching my left hand further into the water, I tried to drag my body towards it by gripping the sand, which only splurted out of the gaps between my fingers. It was useless. Instead, I heaved my body and tried to slide like a worm, but in reality, I was stuck. As I thrashed my feet, claws dug into the bottom of one of them. I grimaced and they switched to my side. All the while it felt as though a heavy object sat on my back. It really was no use. I could not move. And I was sinking.

"No," I cried out. Summoning all my strength, I stretched again. My body writhing, I struggled against my foe and dragged myself forwards, but I moved only centimetres as the grip on my foot was too strong. It was pulling me down, but to where? I had to wake myself. The dark grew thicker, like an impenetrable blanket tumbling from the sky. Soon it would smother everything.

"Come further," the voice whispered in the pitch.

The waves flickered and I stretched out my hand as far as I could, and into something warm, which gripped my wrist and tugged. I felt as if my arm would rip from its socket; such force dragged me towards the water. I struggled, but then the voice told me to be still and not to panic. There was something in the tone that soothed my fears; there was no reason to be afraid.

No reason?! I condemned my reasoning as the icy fingers clasped my feet and dragged me back. Like a ghostly tug of war of invisible forces, they both pulled.

"Let her go," the voice whispered. There was warning in its softness.

I tried to wriggle my feet out of the cold grip once more. It seemed an endless time until I plunged forwards with a jolt. At last the invisible being had released me from its icy embrace, sending me into the water, chilling me to the bone. I drew my legs up towards my body, hugging them to my chest as I sat amongst the waves surrounding me in every direction.

The thing did not follow and I shivered. In front of me I could see clearly, without panic and with grim certainty, that there really was nothing on the beach. Emptiness stretched as far as the eye could see. No footprints. No holes. No evidence of anything. *What was in the sand? Spirits? Clawed demons?* I shivered alone in the dark.

But I was not alone. "Take my hand."

I turned fast and came face to face with a pair of eyes. They stared back, deep and imploring. It was the person I had seen in the sea with dark eyes and even darker hair. He stretched out his hand. "You must come with me or you will surely die here."

"W-who are y-you?" I stammered, shaking with cold. "Where am I? I c-can't swim, I can't..."

"You must."

"No, I'm dreaming. I-I will wake soon." I hugged my feet towards me, wrapping my body against the cold, but I dared not step back on the sand.

"You have no choice," the man said, sounding weary. "I will not let any harm come to you, but you cannot stay here as they will come back."

I looked around, terrified. "Who are *they?*"

There was no reply. Without warning, the stranger's arms encircled my waist and pulled me backwards into the water. As the cold waves swirled around my neck, I screamed, but the silence in the air stifled it. I closed my mouth when salty water swam inside.

"Hold your breath!"

The blanket of dark hovered above my eyes and I felt myself sinking. Strong arms pulled me down into the depths, yet they were warm. I was swept down, down into the dark, into the cold bluest of blues where the water swirled. I closed my eyes in the knowledge that I was going to die, even as I willed myself to wake up. The strangest thing was the sensation of my body evaporating as the depths plunged past me, as though I were descending in some fast, invisible elevator to the end of the world.

The firm arms did not leave my waist as the cool waters pressed against my ears in a never-ending song of silence. I dared not open my eyes, scared of what I might see. Time stopped and yet it seemed to surge on endlessly, and at the point when I thought I could not hold my breath any longer everything else stopped. The arms released me and my legs gave way, but I did not fall. Heavy panting, which I discovered to be the sound of my own breath, filled my ears. My hands felt ground beneath me and I opened my eyelids.

A dark pair of eyes gazed at me quizzically. "How do you feel?"

My lips would not move to answer. I was in shock. He stared and I stared back. *Where am I?* Walls of clear ice shimmered with thousands of cracks of lighter blue amid what resembled white flakes of glistening snow.

The young man squatted down in the space in front of me. Sweeping his long, dark hair behind his ears, he asked me again, "How do you feel?"

"I can breathe," I whispered. Everything felt numb.

He laughed.

I then noticed that his hair was not black at all, but the deepest blue, like the sky beyond the forest. Neither were his eyes so very brown as they were azure; a dim hue like the darkest depths of the sea. *The sea!* I remembered how I had just journeyed through the ocean. It had felt like flying. I jumped up. "Where am I?" I demanded to know. "Who are you? How...?"

"Hold on, no fast movements," the stranger replied,

raising his hand slowly. "Sit down or you may fall."

He was right. I suddenly felt giddy. Before my legs collapsed, I crouched back down. Faintness whizzed through me and the scene blurred before my eyes.

"Don't move," he advised. "Be still. I was worried you might not be able to hold your breath much longer, so I had to swim fast. Perhaps it was too fast. Do you want some water?"

"W-water?" I gasped and almost laughed. I'd had far too much of that. I shook my head. Home was the thing I needed. *Why was I still dreaming?* Perhaps if I hit my head, I'd wake up. I almost died on the beach, so that should have done the trick. I pinched my arm. It hurt, so then I slapped my right cheek, which stung.

It was his turn to jump up in surprise. "What are you doing? You'll hurt yourself!"

"I'm t-trying to w-wake up," I stammered. "I don't like this d-dream anymore."

"You're not asleep," he answered with an edge of merriment. "You're awake, but how did you get on the beach? Where are you from? Did you come from the forest? We haven't seen any survivors in a while..."

"Survivors?" I stared up at him.

Was it my imagination or did his skin seem to shimmer like these walls that resembled frozen water? The wetsuit he wore was of a texture I had never seen before. It was black, but appeared to have scales. They seemed to shift in a silvery wave as he moved and the suit seemed to blend into his skin seamlessly. His feet were bare and pale, but blue? I covered my mouth with my right hand as I tried not to stare.

"From the war," he said. "The Taleryn didn't leave many survivors that we found."

"The Taleryn?" I whispered. My head ached. I buried it in my hands.

"Those on the beach..." The man stopped talking and sat down in front of me, cross-legged, patiently watching. "I think you need to rest. I will request a cabin for you, where you can sleep. I will carry you if you do not feel that you can walk."

I stared at him, but everything started to become hazy and my eyes glazed over. He bent his head towards me and raised my chin, but I was already blacking out, and then everything faded.

Chapter 8

I woke slowly. What a strange dream, or nightmare even, that I had experienced. My head ached as if a vice had been squeezing it during the night. I could feel the blood pumping inside my skull and a chilly draft blew the side of my face. One of the nurses must have left the window ajar. I opened my eyes and time froze. Never before had I been in this room.

The walls simply glistened, like a thousand silver lights dazzling beneath a sheet of sheer ice; flickering so brightly that I squinted as if the sun itself blazed through the windows, but there were none. *This is not a room in the hospital.* I tried to move my toes and they twitched, so I was awake and no longer dreaming, but I could move my feet. *Had my nightmare been real?* I struggled to remember the details. There was definitely a forest and water, and a face...

Everything inside this circular room was blue. There were no bulbs that I could see, but neither were they needed as the flickering from the walls provided more than sufficient light. I was lying on something shaped like a bed, but it was a solid block, albeit soft. It reminded me of the texture of a velvet bag. *The velvet bag!* I suddenly thought of the old woman in the hospital and how she had told me that I would no longer be alone. She had mentioned being woken from... a dream? *No, surely it was sleepwalking? She said she'd been sleepwalking.*

Sitting up, I rubbed my face with my hands and put

my head between my knees. *What was the woman's name? It began with the letter 'S'. Sonia, Sarah? No, Sophia.* She told me she felt sorry for me and gave me a crystal. *The crystal!* The walls drew me; that's why they seemed so familiar – they resembled the crystal! *What did I do with it? In my pocket!* I scrambled with my fingers and, sure enough, I found it in my trousers.

Removing the object, I held it up in the air and gasped at the way it dazzled. Against these starry walls it shone even brighter than before and in the very centre a mist glowed. It almost looked alive. A creeping cold travelled up the back of my neck. *But, surely, if this is a dream..?* I sighed, closing my fist around it. I knew deep down that this was real. Something strange, supernatural even, had occurred and it involved this crystal. *But where am I?*

Stumbling to my feet, I put the mysterious thing back in my pocket, which I zipped up. As I approached the door of the cabin, its solidity gave way. It shimmered and turned to blue mist, which floated in the gap between the walls. I walked through. Turning, I watched it become solid once more. *How strange.* I reached out my fingers to touch the door and once more it became mist. I withdrew my hand and again it solidified.

Glancing around, I found myself in a corridor the colour of a summer sky at home whose walls shone in the same way as those inside the round cabin. I imagined a million fairy lights twinkling all the way along, lighting the route. Beneath my socked feet, the smooth, indigo floor felt oddly warm. I could not see any windows anywhere and the corridor stretched in two directions, so I wandered to the right. My legs felt a little wobbly and I had the now familiar sharp pains as I took each step. It felt like treading on pins, but the experience of walking was such a joy that the discomfort was nothing to me.

The corridor turned and I followed. Now and then I touched the wall, which seemed to glow a darker hue beneath my touch, as though it could sense my fingers hovering. I got the feeling that the walls were somehow alive and then I told my restless imagination to be still.

In a way it felt like I was walking beneath the sea, surrounded as I was by this ghostly blue. The corridor turned once more and then opened up. I staggered and grasped for the wall. Before me there glowed a city, giant, cerulean and glistening. It was inside something resembling a clear, giant bubble. *What lay beyond – the enormity of the sea?* In that moment I thought of the crystal in my pocket, for what I was staring at was reminiscent of its mysterious heart.

Brilliant towers of complex, circular architecture curved upwards from the ground beneath me. From where I stood there descended a flight of steps, sinking all the way down to a maze of walkways far below, between which water flowed. At the other side were more tall structures, shimmering like the walls of the corridor, resembling glass.

I was in a world seemingly carved of crystal and filled with blue mist. Far below, in the distance, I could make out minute figures walking around. A grey coloured tail flipped out of the water and then plopped back in as people clothed in the colours of the ocean strode along the walkways, oblivious to the spectacle. Calm water stretched out towards the edges of the dome, which was immense. I could not begin to guess its width or height, or how many people could possibly live here. In the air, creatures flew, or did they? I squinted. Where I expected to see birds, tiny silver fish glided along. I gazed, spellbound as they swam in the mist that filled the entire dome.

Chapter 9

My legs gave way and I sat down. From the walkways down below, many long flights of steps led up to gaps in the corridor I had walked through. I assumed the area was full of living quarters, just like the one where I had slept. Astonished, I remained still and surveyed, wide-eyed this city or world – I didn't know what to call it; I only knew that it was so dazzlingly beautiful. There was neither sun nor moon nor stars, only this faint mist. The stars of my home had been replaced by the glittering lights that flickered in the blue of everything. It was truly wondrous.

"Did you sleep well?"

The words startled me. Turning my head, I recognised the young man from my nightmare, or rather from yesterday if this were not a dream. He was the one who had rescued me from the invisible beings on the beach. I shivered at the memory. The stranger was smiling, but in a slightly awkward way.

I wrapped my hands more closely around my legs as the youth crouched down ever so slowly. His long hair was dark indigo, as were his eyes, which glinted, and I noticed how his skin had a strange pale blue sheen. He was no longer wearing the wetsuit of before, but clothes. *Of course they had to be blue.* The material was not one that I recognised. This stranger wore long trousers and a sleeveless top that reached below his waist. His build was quite muscular, but slim, and his jaw line sharp. A necklace of fine beads, reminiscent of the sea, was fastened around his neck and I noticed matching cords wrapped several times around his wrists.

I smiled to myself. *Was everything here blue, like the sea?* On his feet the man wore some kind of thick-soled shoe. Again the material was unknown to me, but resembled woven strands of greenish algae. I tried to guess the age of this man who looked to be not much older than me. In the end I decided on twenty to twenty-two, but I could not be sure. For all I knew, time might be different in this place.

"You do not feel like talking?" he asked, bending down so that his eyes were on a level with my own. He followed my gaze, which darted to and fro across the scenery below. "I imagine this is a lot to take in," he said, gesturing. "This is Entyre. This is my home and where I was born. There are about a million of us living here. We are known as the Keepers of the Deep. My name is Skyen." He smiled and then fell silent, as if waiting for my response.

I swallowed. "That's quite an introduction," I replied, hugging my knees. "Where are we... exactly?"

"Ah," he sighed, leaning back with a slight frown. "You have not heard of Entyre?"

"No," I replied, knowing he would not have heard of my home either. That is, if I really wasn't dreaming. I was not sure of anything anymore.

"We were watching the shoreline, as we do every night, looking for survivors of the war and monitoring the activities of the Taleryn. They were the ones who attacked you. Their race is destructive, insatiable, and their hunger cannot be quenched. So far they have not found a way to enter the sea. It destroys them."

"I could not see them," I murmured, remembering the icy touch and sharp claws with a shiver.

Skyen nodded. "We cannot see them either."

"So, how..."

"We can hear them. Did you not hear the wailing?" he asked.

Recalling the haunting sound, I nodded.

"Their wails drown out all noise," he continued. "Where they are is silent except for their voices. After a while, survivors say they cannot hear their own minds."

I shuddered, recalling how I had tried to scream, but the sound vanished, sucked away by the darkness.

"I called out to you on the beach and I brought you here. Do you remember swimming down through the waves?" asked Skyen.

"Yes, I do. It was frightening. I don't like water..."

"Really? I am surprised. We love it. We are one. The sea is in all of us and we are in it."

My eyes widened in panic. "Are we still in the sea?" I asked, not sure if I wanted to know the answer. I could see water beyond the edge of the dome, but the fact did not jell with my own definition of reality.

Skyen nodded. "Yes, this city is under the ocean. In this globe there is sufficient oxygen for us to breathe. Our people have lived here for thousands of years. Where are you from? I have never seen anyone with hair so red or skin so white."

I pushed my hair back behind my ears, self-consciously aware of the penetrating blaze of his stare. The man seemed to look straight through me. I imagined he could read my thoughts, but then I realised that he clearly could not if he was asking questions.

"My name is Jayne," I replied, and then I lied because it was easier, "I don't know where I am from. My head aches. I can't remember anything before the forest." I looked away, fearful that he would detect somehow that I was not being truthful, although it was a kind of truth as this reality had begun among those trees beneath that darkened sky.

"That is to be expected, I guess," he said softly. "This must all be a lot for you."

I nodded. There was a kindness in the man's eyes that made me look away. I gazed around at the city spread out before me, which seemed to sparkle. All around, the familiar blue mist filled the air and it carried the scent of the sea. It brought to mind the memory of being by the ocean on a stormy day in the past. When it roared and crashed against the rocks, I had tasted salt on my lips, and this smelt like that. While everything was strange and perplexing to me, the ghostly mist was calming and oddly familiar, but I could not fathom why.

"Do you feel like walking?" asked Skyen after a while.

I glanced at the man who seemed to be extremely patient, knowing that I must appear to be a very strange creature and something of a mystery. I was becoming increasingly self-conscious of my flame-red hair and green eyes, and unique clothing. I was not going to be able to wander around without drawing attention to myself. Part of me wanted to hide. *Were these people friendly? What will they think of me, a stranger?*

"I don't know," I replied honestly. "Does everyone here look like you, with blue hair, eyes and..."

"Skin?" asked Skyen, completing the sentence. He smiled. "Yes, they do. As I told you, we are one with the sea. But we welcome strangers. Difference is not something we fear."

My companion stood up and held out his hand. I looked at the back of my own alabaster-white hand and back to his, which had the palest blue sheen. It was so unreal.

"If you would like, I can show you my home," he continued with a smile. "You are welcome here, as are all survivors."

I stared up, wondering how he could he be so trusting. For all he knew, I might cause him harm. This must be a peaceful people, I surmised. Sighing, I took his hand, expecting it to be cold, like water, but to my surprise it was warmer than mine.

"Don't let go of my hand and I will walk you down these steps," he said, protectively. "They may be a bit steep for you. There is no need to fear this place or the people here."

I let him lead me down the stairway to the walkway that crossed the expanse of sea within the dome. I marvelled at the calmness of the waves inside. All of the people were taller than me and had various shades of blue hair. I noticed how some had eyes that were even darker than Skyen's. Everyone stared as they passed, but smiled warmly at the same time. They appeared to welcome outsiders, or rather survivors, which is what they evidently presumed me to be. None of them looked troubled by my appearance, although one or two stopped to gaze blatantly at my fiery hair. It must have looked astonishingly bright against the blue of everything else.

As we walked I frowned slightly at the sharp pricks in the soles of my feet, but tried to focus on Skyen's words as he pointed out the numerous buildings and various sections of this part of the city. There did not appear to be any mode of transport that I could see. All of the people simply walked.

In that instant I thought of Michael. How would he feel when he found out that I was missing? A stab of guilt plunged into the pit of my stomach, stealing my breath away for a second. I wondered exactly how long I had been away – would it be just one night or longer? *How will I get home?* The thought leapt to the front of my mind and I flung it to the back, fearful that I might begin to panic.

I had to remain calm, whatever happened. I was still not convinced that I was not dreaming... somehow. Perhaps the nurses had given me the wrong medication. *Will night and day, and time, be the same here beneath this blue globe?* I tried to calm my jitters, but it was no good. A hundred scenarios stirred up in my fertile imagination, each one worse than the last.

"This is the Centre of Knowing," announced Skyen.

Stopping, I realised that I had been so wrapped up in my thoughts that I had not noticed the tall building in front of us. It resembled the spiral trunk of tree in which there was an entrance. I followed my guide through the doorway, which shimmered into mist, vanished, and then reappeared after we had entered. The room within was the opposite of what I had imagined. Inside was monstrously huge and round in shape. It reminded me of a library, but one that lacked any books.

"These are the Knowing," explained Skyen, picking up a thin blue piece of something resembling ice. He held it up to me. "Look into it."

The sheet looked as blue as a summer sky, but then

it cleared, and I could see pictures and people. *How is it possible?*

"This will teach you our history," Skyen explained. "This place is full of the Knowing. I can show you many things about our city, our people and our history."

I blinked. It was too much to take in. It was exciting, but I felt numb from exhaustion and fear. I yearned to sleep and wake up back home with the familiar.

Skyen smiled and I felt guilty for not sharing his excitement. "I can see you are too tired," he said. "This is all too much for you and I should have thought better of bringing you here. I understand. I think it is time for you to eat something and sleep. Tomorrow I will take you to meet the Balaenoptera. All newcomers must be greeted. Don't be afraid, Jayne. I can see your fear and it need not be."

I could not help but smile as my companion's grin was oddly contagious. I allowed him to take my hand and guide me sleepily back to my blue-filled cabin.

Chapter 10

Drifting out of sleep, I felt an oddly familiar draft on my face as I opened my eyes. I was lying on a soft pillow, which smelt slightly lemony, on a solid block of a bed, covered in blue blankets that felt like velvet. All around the bed was a dark blue curtain. Pushing my hair back from my face, I sat up. Finding a gap in the curtain, I dragged it across so that I could step out.

All around the walls shimmered like silver lights under a sheet of blue glass. I closed my eyes, perplexed, and then I remembered the unbelievable happenings of the previous day. *Was this lucid dream still continuing? Was my addled brain conjuring up dreams within dreams?* I opened my eyes again, but nothing changed. The walls continued to flicker.

Remembering that my legs worked in this strange reality, I stood up. Deciding to make the best of the situation, I wiped the sleep from my eyes and looked around. If this was a dream, I was going to enjoy it; if it was not, I would try to do the same while working out how to get back home.

The cabin was of average size and round. I saw an image of a girl with red hair and realised it was my own reflection in a clear column of ice in the centre of the room. What a cool mirror, I thought, walking towards it. Reaching out my fingers, I found it cold to touch. My crazy looking hair was in dire need of a comb and I suddenly missed my belongings at home. I was still wearing my clothes from the day before, and I felt hot and sticky.

Reaching into the right-hand pocket of my black trousers, I felt the hard edge of the crystal, and in a flash I recalled it slicing my hand and a bright light blinding me. *Had it really brought me here?* I shook my head at my reflection. The idea was nonsensical, but then so was everything else. Waving my hand in the air, I dismissed my image and took a closer look around the room.

One side was covered with what resembled shelves, except they were not straight and looked to be made of ice. They felt firm and not as cold as the mirror. I recognised the books, or rather blue ice sheets, which I had seen in the round room inside the tree.

Further along were a few objects that looked familiar; variations on a theme, as they were close to what I knew, but slightly different. There was a comb and a small mirror, resembling some kind of frozen ice inside a blue material of some kind, and a toothbrush and a pot of something that smelt like sea salt. A pile of soft blue cloths and a bottle of clear liquid sat nearby. There was also a plate of fruit and vegetables. I picked at the blue-green coloured grapes, which melted in my mouth, before taking the comb and tidying my hair.

Turning, I noticed a soft-looking, blue chair and a table that appeared to be made of ice. I supposed the material just resembled it, because how could it be so without melting? The thought made me frown. Spotting a cupboard, I opened the doors wide to discover a rail supporting a few items of clothing and some drawers full of undergarments, even socks.

Everything was familiar, yet slightly different and made of unknown substances.

I had an idea. Removing the crystal from my pocket, I held it up in the air. It evoked an eerie feeling inside me as it seemed to be alive. Catching sight of the mist-covered city in the centre, a chill ran down my back. Sitting down, I removed one of my socks and placed the crystal inside. Then I placed it at the back of the wardrobe. Removing the rest of my clothes, I placed them on top. The thing was now hidden.

Checking through the garments on the clothes rail, I chose a long blue skirt and sleeveless top, which appeared to be of the right size. Draping them on the back of the chair, I noticed a pair of sandals on the floor near the door. They had thick soles and the material looked like woven strands of algae, similar to Skyen's footwear, but more feminine. Skyen! The man's face appeared in my mind and I remembered him guiding me around a small part of the city; the stranger who had rescued me. Recalling the swim down through the ocean, I shook my head. Everything was too unbelievable.

Opening the drawers in the cupboard, I pulled out some underwear and placed them on the chair. I was about to put them on when I realised that I was far too dirty to wear all of these clean things. There had to be somewhere to wash. Looking around, I spied a door that I had not noticed before. At my approach it shimmered into nothing.

I found myself in a room decorated with transparent white tiles, resembling cuts of sheer ice. It was beautiful. The room contained a bath tub with odd curves, which seemed to mould itself into the floor, a shower of sorts, a toilet and a sink. Everything seemed to be made of some ice-like material, but it was tough. Noticing a series of buttons by the shower, I pressed them all until I accomplished a steady flow of warm water, and I stepped beneath it. A series of round-shaped balls of what I guessed to be something like soap sat waiting on the side.

Gazing up at the single head from which the water poured, I closed my eyes and relaxed. It cascaded down my hair and body, trickling into a small hole on the floor. I remained in that position until I noticed my fingertips looking like prunes. Laughing, I gathered up a ball of soap and washed. Seeing nothing that resembled shampoo, I used the same, and then dried myself using one of the blue cloths sitting in a pile on an icy shelf. The room was perfect. Feeling rejuvenated, I wandered out with my hair wrapped up.

After dressing, I turned to check my reflection in the mirror and found the clothes to be a perfect fit. Uncannily, someone had guessed correctly. Skyen was good with garments, I thought with a smile. The sleeveless top was long, slim fitting and felt soft, the material being very fine indeed. The skirt, of the same shade and fabric, trailed an inch or so above my ankles. Sitting down on the bed, I dried my hair and combed it out again until a loud knock disturbed me.

Smoothing down my unruly hair, which always seemed to have a life of its own, I walked towards the door, which shimmered to nothing. Skyen stood in the doorway wearing a shy expression.

"Hello," I said, brushing my slightly damp hair back from my face.

"You look fresher today," he remarked, "and the clothes fit?"

"Yes," I replied, smiling. "They are perfect and the shower is awesome."

"Awesome?"

"I mean wonderful. You guessed my size correctly," I added, slipping my feet into the sandals.

Skyen laughed. "That was not my doing. Syla, my sister, chose them for you. She brought them in while you were sleeping. Nothing was going to wake you, she said."

"I did sleep really well," I agreed. "But I still think I'm dreaming and you're not real, but I'm going to play along and pretend."

The man frowned and scratched the side of his head. "As you wish."

A long silence followed, which I decided to break by asking, "Am I going to meet your sister?"

Skyen's face broke into a grin. "Soon, but first I must take you to meet the Balaenoptera, the Rulers of the Deep. All newcomers must be greeted."

"Oh, yes, I remember you told me this yesterday. Are they scary men?"

"No, not really," Skyen replied, shaking his head. "Come now, if you are ready."

Nodding, I followed my guide out into the blue corridor. The walls glimmered eerily, lighting the way like a million fairy lights, but I was getting used to it, just as I was beginning to not notice the tiny pains in the soles of my feet. The sandals felt soft and comfortable. Skyen led me to the right and we headed towards the steps that led down into the glorious city.

Chapter 11

Skyen stopped in front of a tall, familiar-looking spiral trunk. The Centre of Knowing looked exactly the same as it had the day before, so at least my coma-induced, imaginative fantasy was consistent, I thought. I studied my guide and followed him through the mist and into the gigantic room beyond. We crossed the grey, stone floor to the very centre on which there appeared to be a round, blue disc. Upon reaching it, I noticed it was not solid at all. Instead it contained the same glowing mist as every other door I had seen.

"What's down there?" I asked.

"The Balaenoptera," Skyen replied.

I shifted my feet backwards and peered down. "Are we allowed to go in?"

"Yes. As soon as you entered the city, your presence was known to them. We are expected, so the way is open."

"I expected a guard or something," I said, peering down the hole.

Skyen laughed. "They do not need protection. They fear no one."

"I see," I answered, feeling embarrassed. "Are they gods or kings?"

"Not exactly. Come. I will show you."

Skyen stepped through the blue and his body gradually disappeared, but with this entrance the mist remained. With some trepidation, I followed and found myself stepping down some steps that seemed to appear out of nowhere. They looked to be made of frozen ice, but felt as solid as stone beneath my feet.

Skyen walked in front of me and there was a slight chill in the air. We were in a huge expanse of dark indigo space, lit by stars in the walls. It was also round in shape and I presumed we must be walking under Entyre, where I had expected the sea to be. The globe must be even more enormous than it seemed from above, I thought, stepping carefully as there was no rail to grip. I was suddenly grateful that I did not suffer from vertigo, for the staircase began very high and it was a long way down.

"Are you okay?" asked my guide, turning around.

I nodded. "I'm fine. Where are we?"

"Beneath the city," he replied, leaving me none the wiser.

We continued our slow pace down the stairway until we reached the bottom. When I looked back up, the circular entrance was but a tiny pinpoint in the dim light. Beneath my feet, the ground resembled frozen, pale blue ice. In that split second I realised it was sheer and that I could see the ocean beneath. I tried to rein in my terror of water and glanced everywhere else but down. The construction of the place was huge; the furthest sides to my north, east and west blurred in the distance.

"There is nothing to fear," said Skyen, noticing my expression.

"I'm scared of water," I replied.

"I know."

Taking my hand, the man led me slowly across the frozen floor, which abruptly gave way to dark waves. I jolted, stepping back, but Skyen did not let go of my hand. In that moment something grey and shiny rose up into the air, and sank back down again, splashing us.

"A dolphin!" I gasped, laughing.

"Yes, there are many here," Skyen replied, amazed at my response.

"I love them. I went to see some once when I was younger, with my parents," I recalled and then paused at the memory. "They were trained to..."

"Trained? How?"

"The dolphin trainers taught them to do tricks, and jump through hoops and things..."

Skyen frowned. "But that is wrong. Dolphins are wild and free; an intelligent race. I do not believe they could be trained to do what humans tell them."

Not wanting to upset him, I replied, "They're my favourite animal, so beautiful."

Nodding, he took my hand, and led me backwards as another three dolphins leapt out of the water, followed by an expanse of grey-blue that seemed to go on forever. The whale reared up in the air in front of me, seeming to fill the space beneath the city. Droplets rushed off of him, splashing into the water below. I both feared and was impressed by the sheer power of the creature. The otherworldly sounds it made were indescribable.

Feeling Skyen's eyes burning into the side of my face, I turned to him. He stifled laughter, I thought, as I imagined my face was a picture at that moment. "The Balaenoptera," he informed me.

The whale, having launched itself into the air, was motionless. Barnacles sparkled all over its surface and water rushed down. The very air seemed full of awe.

"I welcome you to Entyre."

Glancing at Skyen, I saw that his lips were closed. He had not said a word. "I heard a voice," I began.

He nodded at the creature in front of us and I frowned as I gazed up at it. *How was it possible? Some kind of telepathy?* Unconsciously, I stepped backwards.

"Do not be afraid. I welcome you. Where are you from?"

"It asked me a question," I whispered.

"So answer it."

I pulled a face at Skyen. "How?"

"Well, you could say the words aloud or you could just think them."

Think them? I looked back at the giant whale in front of me as cascades of water swept down its sides. "I was on the beach by the forest and found myself wandering among the trees. I was rescued from the things in the sand. They were invisible," I blurted out.

"The Taleryn are our mortal enemy. You were lucky to escape them. Many are not so lucky," replied the voice in my head.

"Skyen rescued me. He brought me here."

"We have seen much of Skyen's bravery. We watch him with interest. His father was a brave human also."

Although my companion would have no idea what the voice was telling me, he looked at me quizzically. "He says your father was a brave man," I told him.

Skyen looked down and nodded. "He was."

Wondering what had happened to him, I thought it best not to ask. Instead, I listened to my mind: "Where are you from?"

"From the forest," I said, not knowing how to answer.

"I do not conceive it to be so," came the reply.

I blinked. *How did it know?* "I come from a different land," I explained. "It is not far."

"Where are you from?" asked the voice again. "You will have to tell me if you wish to remain here in Entyre."

Trembling, I glanced sidelong at Skyen, but he was focused on the whale. I had no idea what to say as the truth would sound incredulous. Deciding not to speak out loud, I concentrated my thoughts in reply. I described my accident, the old woman who visited me in the hospital and gave me the crystal, and how I had found myself in the forest and able to walk, thinking that I was dreaming; then followed my journey through the trees and to the beach, the horror and my rescue, and the long swim down to this city.

When I finished, I noticed that Skyen was watching me intently. The silence was broken by the shimmer of a dolphin leaping through the air and splashing back down into the depths of the sea.

"This is the truth I seek," said the voice in my head. "You are not the first. The power of the crystal is strong. It is a great gift that you have regained the freedom to use your body to the full; so great a gift should always be repaid."

I gasped. *Repaid how?*

"Time is all we have," continued the voice. "You are welcome in Entyre for however long you wish to stay. We only ask that you abide by our ways. How you live your life shall be reflected back to you in the waters. I have one warning for you: do not break the crystal unless you wish to breathe here no more."

My mind leapt to the piece of glass hidden in my clothes at the back of the wardrobe. So that was the way back home, I now knew. I only had to smash the thing; it was that easy. I almost laughed at the realisation.

"I bid you leave," said the voice and the mighty Balaenoptera slowly descended into the waves. Water flooded the ground and over our feet as the creature disappeared into the darkness.

"You did well," Skyen remarked. He smiled warmly and I found myself feeling embarrassed under his stare.

"He welcomed me," I replied. "I guess it was a 'he'. It was a male voice, but it was so strange. The voice was in my head. It was as if I was thinking each word, but I knew it wasn't me."

"Yes, I remember being afraid the first time."

"Have you been down here a lot?" I asked.

"I've spoken to the Balaenoptera a number of times," Skyen replied with a shrug, "but they are not the only ones who communicate by telepathy. Our ancestors do."

"Your ancestors?"

"Yes, our ancestors return to the sea when they pass on. Only those who have not led worthy lives remain on land."

"What happens to them?" I asked.

"There is still a commemoration of their passing, but we burn their bodies. They remain rooted to the earth, but our people dream to return to the sea. The worthy succeed."

"I don't understand."

"You will," Skyen said, smiling. "Our traditions sound impossible or strange, I imagine. I want to know what you replied. Why did you not speak it aloud, the place from hence you came?"

Biting my lip, I was stumped for words. Something warned me not to tell him. "I can't talk about it."

"I'm sorry," he said with a hint of sadness on his face. "I did not mean to pry or remind you of difficult times."

"It's fine," I replied.

"So I am forgiven?"

"Of course," I answered, and my words were returned by a warm smile, which made me blush. I turned my face sideways to hide the creeping redness and walked a little way ahead.

"Come, we should ascend and then we can explore some more, if you wish," he suggested.

I turned with a smile. "What is your name?"

He laughed. "You know it."

"Your whole name. I just realised I don't know."

"Skyen Yij Arind Lanyajigan."

I giggled. "I can't even pronounce that."

"You asked me."

"Okay, cool. Now that I know who you are, we can go now!"

Skyen chuckled, somewhat mystified. "And what is cool?"

"It means great," I translated, "but better."

"Cool," said Skyen, trying the word for size and seeming to like it. "You climb up first. Then if you slip, I can catch you. It's a long way down."

"I have no intention of looking down," I replied, laughing. "At all."

The ascent passed much more quickly than the reverse and we were soon in the Centre of Knowing.

Chapter 12

The next week passed in a whirl, during which Skyen turned up every day to show me around the city and teach me something new about the ways of his people. Since discovering how I could get home, I thought constantly about the crystal, but so far I had delayed smashing it. Every day I remembered my other home, Michael, my grandfather, Charlotte and my friends, and other relatives. But for some reason I delayed. The adventure I was having was too thrilling to end yet. I wanted to explore a little more before going back.

The week culminated with Skyen inviting me to his family's cabin for dinner. All day, I was consumed by nervousness, although I was very eager to meet his sister. I imagined that I would have much in common with her somehow. The only thing I dreaded was being asked questions regarding my home, for I had no idea how to respond.

"Everyone, this is Jayne," announced Skyen as I trailed behind him into the sky-coloured room where lights glistened in the walls and all of the furnishings were a deep indigo. An array of faces leapt up from the glass table to greet me.

An elderly lady took my hands and smiled intently at me. I noticed her fingers were decorated with many silver rings with various sea-coloured stones. "Welcome. I am Eleva and this is my mate, Jayeb," she said.

Jayeb, a tall, thin man who wore spectacles, smiled

thinly and held out a trembling hand, which I shook. I wondered how old he was.

The couple took their seats as a younger woman with long, flowing hair hugged me. "I am Hena, Skyen's aunt. And this is my mate, Bastian. Skyen's late father was his brother."

So his father is dead. Skyen's expression did not reveal a thing.

"I am Steden, another uncle," said a sturdy man with a firm handshake.

"And I am Syla," announced a girl who looked very similar to Skyen, though several years younger. "I am the little sister," she revealed with a grin.

I laughed as she was much taller than me, slim and willowy, with long, fine hair that fell to her waist. It hung in two long plaits.

"It's lovely to meet you all," I said shyly, slightly overcome by all of the people.

"This is my friend, Yava," Syla continued.

The other girl stepped forward. Her aquamarine hair hung to her waist, but it was decorated with delicate flowers. Her skin was very white, like ice, her eyes clear and pale, and she was extremely beautiful. "Hello," she said.

"Nice to meet you," I replied, in awe of her physical perfection. I watched the girl take her seat at the table with the rest of the family, and she seemed to glide.

"These last two are my friends, Foien and Estoyib," said Skyen. "The intelligent one is Foien and the crazy one is Estoyib!"

"Hey!" cried the latter in protest. "Just because I do not conform to what everyone thinks I should be doing with my life does not mean that I am crazy."

"I agree," I said, to my surprise.

"Aha!" gasped Foien with a grin. "See, I like her already! A girl after my own heart."

"I hope not," Skyen answered with a nervous laugh.

I watched him walk towards the table, wondering what he meant by that. Foien gave me a knowing look and then shrugged. There was one empty chair at the table, in between Skyen's grandparents, so I took it and tried to make myself feel at ease.

Sitting down, I realised that the table was not glass, but made of some kind of sheer ice. Wooden cutlery sat waiting beside a cloth napkin. The bowls and glasses were of something resembling blue glass. I peered at one of my two cups, which was full of a translucent liquid.

"It is lemon water, my child," explained Evela. "Skyen said you are not from the city?"

My heart sank at the dreaded question. "That is true. I am from another place, quite far away," I answered honestly. "He rescued me from the beach."

"So you are a survivor of the war," stated Yayeb. It was not a question.

I did not correct his false assumption, but nodded as I took a sip of my drink, which was cool and refreshing. It tasted like water with a squeeze of lemon, but mixed with something else that I could not put my finger on. It would come to me in time, I suspected.

"How did you colour your hair?" asked Syla. "It is so different."

All eyes turned to me in anticipation of the answer. From the opposite end of the table, Skyen winked at me. Slightly taken aback, I felt myself blush as I considered my reply. The best policy was to be truthful. Then and there, I decided that I would dodge all questions regarding where I was from, but answer all others as honestly as I could, without shocking anyone or sounding completely mad.

"It's natural," I replied.

"But how?" asked Syla. "Everyone's hair is a shade of blue, from light to dark, while the elders have grey."

"Where I come from we don't live in the water," I explained.

"Oh," said Foien. "So you live on land?"

I nodded. "Yes. Many people have hair like mine, but the most common colour is brown."

"Brown?" asked Evela. "That is very boring!"

Syla giggled, which rippled like a breeze on the surface of a lake. Estoyib stared at her from under his eyelashes for quite a while and I detected more than friendly interest in them. Syla was oblivious to the attention though as she took a sip of her lemon water.

"How do you find our city?" asked Yava, turning her clear eyes on me.

"I like it very much," I replied warmly. "It is very beautiful and I've seen nothing like it ever before."

"Do you think you will make it your home?" she questioned and I thought I saw her eyes narrow.

"Perhaps," I replied, although I still planned to go home as soon as I could and escape this strange, dreamlike world.

"Jayne has only just got here," Skyen remarked. "It is too soon to ask such questions. I will ask Manna to bring in the food."

I was thankful he had changed the subject. Smiling at me, he got up and walked towards a doorway to the left. The mist within shimmered and he was gone. As I looked back at the table, I noticed Yava's beautiful eyes on me. Detected, she turned to Syla quickly and started to make conversation.

"You will enjoy this, I think," said Evela. "Manna is a talented preparer of food."

"Ah, yes, all her dishes are wonderful," added Jayeb as his eyes washed over with happiness. "I live for these meals."

"Old man, you are funny!" laughed Evela, nudging him behind my back.

"Dear, you have to live for something," he answered slowly, his face trembling slightly as he spoke. Again I wondered exactly how old he was. Quite a few years older than his wife, I guessed.

"You should be living for me," Evela retorted in protest, "of course!"

The old man shrugged. "But I do, every single day!"

As I giggled, Skyen walked in beside a short woman whom I assumed to be Manna. Carrying various dishes, they walked to and fro a few times before Skyen finally took his seat and the lady disappeared back through the doorway.

"Is she not eating with us?" I asked.

"She prefers to eat in the food-preparation rooms," advised Jayeb.

"Yes, Manna knows she can eat here, but she does not choose to. She is not a servant," added Evela, passing me a dish. "Try this. It is made with a variety of fruits and pastry. Wonderful it is. And you must try this carrot, almond and apple dish."

"Thank you," I told her, spooning some of the concoction on to my plate. A delicious aroma wafted up and I felt my appetite rush over me. For the next ten minutes there was silence as everyone tucked into their food. Evela was right: it tasted wonderful.

Afterwards, Syla and Skyen cleared the table, and their grandparents retired to their room. Everyone else seated themselves and relaxed.

"How about we get some air?" Skyen asked me. "The stars are out. You can see them through the globe outside."

"But we are under the water. How is it possible?" I asked.

"Magic," he replied.

"Have you not seen that yet?" asked Syla, grasping her hands together.

I shook my head. "No, I haven't been here long."

"Well, you must see it - simply beautiful. We should all go," she suggested, glancing around.

Skyen's auntie and uncles opted to stay home while the rest of us left the cabin. We headed down the winding corridor and towards the nearest flight of steps in order to descend. As we turned a corner, the space opened up and I was greeted by glowing stars. They seemed to glitter more brightly than those of home, but it was a trick of the eye. These stars were embedded in the globe surrounding the city. It was only that they glowed by night. Below, all else sparkled.

"It is wonderful," I gasped.

"Told you," said Skyen, taking my hand, which, to my surprise, I welcomed.

I wondered if he was only being protective or if there was more to it, but I could not read his face. His action did not go unnoticed by his two friends who nudged one another while his sister smiled and discreetly looked away. I could not read Yava's expression as she kept her head turned, but I was sure she studied me out of the corner of her eye. Her lips were tightly pursed and her demeanour as still as the grave.

Skyen led me down the steps, one by one, with his family and friends following behind us. This city was spellbinding, lying here beneath the ocean. The thought seemed to sink into my mind and cement itself, as though I had been denying it before: we were beneath the waves and everything, down in the heart of the sea.

I was not dreaming. There was no way that my imagination could conjure all of this up and for it to seem so real. As I felt my fingers being gently squeezed by this man's warm hand, I finally knew it was really happening. I would not wake. If I did, I would always wake here. Somehow it did not frighten me.

"I love this walk down here at night," said Syla to me. "If you listen, you can hear the whale song. Can you hear it, Jayne?"

I concentrated, but could only hear the soft buzz of distant conversations. "No, I can only hear the people."

"Ah, maybe you need to be here for a while to grow accustomed to them. It is one of my earliest memories, the song of the whales. It is loudest here at night time. It soothes me to sleep sometimes," Syla added, her voice growing soft.

I turned and she smiled at me. "I hope you will love it here, as I do," she said brightly.

"Thank you," I replied, noticing that Yava did not meet my eyes this time. She stared into the distance at a spot beyond me. I wondered why she was so closed. *How could anyone so beautiful be so shy of others?*

Chapter 13

The following weeks sped by and I gradually became more used to the sight of the ocean and the blue mist that seemed to follow me everywhere, and even the tiny fish that swam through the air all around. Enjoying every day that passed, I forgot about the crystal at the back of my closet and tried not to think about the people I had left behind in my other world. At the moment this one seemed more real to me, and I felt more independent and alive here.

Hearing a knock outside my door, I leapt up from my bed and rushed over. The blue mist softened and disappeared as I stepped within it.

"Hello."

It was Skyen. The huge smile on his face was contagious and I blushed as my fingers trembled against my dress. My constant guide was growing on me, steadily and surely. He was the last person I spoke to before going to sleep and the first one I seemed to see each morning. If I left this place I would miss him. I knew this and it frightened me. I did not wish my decision to be taken out of my hands by some emotion, but I knew it to be true. I was afraid that I could not leave now because however much I tried to argue, my growing feelings for him would not allow me to go.

"Are you well?" he asked.

"Yes, yes," I mumbled. "I was just daydreaming,

thinking. You know, the way I do. Always my mind is thinking of something."

"I find it interesting," he replied, watching me as I gathered my things into my small bag and slipped on my sandals. "I can empty my mind completely."

"Ah, I wish I could. Okay, I've got everything in my bag, so where are you taking me today?"

"Surprise," he answered, taking my hand.

I felt a familiar wave in my stomach as I walked beside him, our fingers entwined. We trod the curving corridor until we came to the steps that crept down to the walkway far below. My breath caught in my throat as my eyes caught the spectacular view once again and I wondered if I would ever grow accustomed to it. Smiling, I followed Skyen down the long flight of steps, gazing out across the blue city beneath this world of icy glass.

"You seem very happy this morning," Skyen remarked as we reached the first walkway.

"I am. Is that bad?" I asked with a sly grin.

"Of course not, it is good. I am happy."

"I think I may be getting used to this place..."

"So you don't want to leave?" he asked.

"Why?"

"I thought you'd want to return to your people."

"You think I may have got bored of all the blue?" I joked.

My companion laughed, but then his eyes turned serious. "I am glad you are in no hurry to leave. I would have taken you myself, back to the forest, and helped you to find your people."

"Thank you, although I think they would have been difficult to find..."

"Is that the reason you stay?"

I shook my head. "No, I like it here."

"And do you like me?"

I stopped and tried to meet his gaze, but found that I could not. As the blood rushed to my face, I glanced away. When I turned back, Skyen was still staring at me. I nodded shyly, and he laughed, so I nudged him and pretended to run away. Of course, he followed, but upon catching up with me, he grabbed me around the waist and lifted me high in the air, not caring at the looks upon the faces of those passing by, who suddenly stared at us.

Giggling, I pounded on Skyen's arms with my fists, but he did not set me down. Instead he turned around again, staring up at me so that I was forced to look down at him. Our eyes met and he gently lowered me to the ground. I froze in the moment, unable to do anything, confused by the myriad reflections rushing through my mind, soon cast out by one single thought that seemed to consume me. *Am I in love?* I tried to push it down, but it was no use. As he brushed the hair back from my face and touched the curve of my chin, I knew I was lost. I knew I was staying and would never leave as long as I enjoyed being with him.

"Come," he said, breaking away, "before we shrivel under all these stares."

Taking my hand, Skyen led me along the walkway, which twisted between deep pools of water. We walked as far as possible until we came to the edge of things; the end of this world. Ahead, stretching as far as the eye could see, or mine at least, was the ocean, so mysterious and beautiful.

I inhaled deeply, as if I could breathe in the salt

that lingered in the air and inside the ethereal mist. *I could stay here, I could.* There was something eternally peaceful about the sea. If only I could combat my fear of it. My body, as though remembering, yearned to swim, but my irrational phobia prevented me. I wondered if it would always be so. To be afraid of something I used to love so much seemed too cruel.

"Does it make you sad?" he asked, as though reading my thoughts.

"No, no," I said, turning to face him. "I love it. I'm just scared, that's all. It's so beautiful."

"Do you think one day you will want to swim there?"

"I hope so. I remember that I once loved it."

"My ancestors are there," he continued, waving his hand towards the water.

"All of them?" I blurted out, and then felt stupid.

He laughed. "Yes, where are yours?"

"Erm, dead."

"But where?"

I bit my lip. "They're buried in graveyards... in the ground. Is that what you're asking?" I replied.

"All of them?" he asked, frowning.

I nodded.

"But that is so depressing, so final. To be enclosed in the heavy earth..." He shivered, before turning back to look out at the endless, fathomless ocean. "That is where I will go in the end, to become one with the sea."

"Do you believe that?"

"Yes, of course, because it is true. The dolphins that you see here, they are our ancestors. The whales are the Rulers of the Deep, but they were not always so. They were once human too."

"I see you really believe it," I observed. "It isn't just a story or a religion?"

"Religion?"

"Hmm, I mean a belief in a god or something. You know, or a ruler who is not human, kind of."

"Like the Balaenoptera," he surmised. "But, yes, I believe. That is why it is important that we live our life according to the codes of peacefulness and truth, for we wish to return to the sea."

"It is perfectly calm out there," I commented, changing the subject, which I could not understand. I was amazed at Skyen's blind belief in something so mystical and outrageous. My parents had not believed in any religion, so I had not been brought up to have any faith in one.

"Can you hear them?" he asked.

"Who?"

"The Balaenoptera, of course. Can you hear their song?"

I shook my head, sadly.

"Listen more closely. Close your eyes and let your imagination drift."

"Drift?"

"Out on the waves," Skyen replied, and I thought I could hear amusement in his voice.

I kept my eyes shut and concentrated. All I could hear was the trickle of water and the voices of people a short distance away. Focusing on my own breathing, I tried to shut them out, pushing away the sounds of everything else, and then I concentrated on the silence, trying to penetrate it. As the other noises fell away, I sensed something else; a vibration in the air. It was like a ringing sound, but only for a second, and then it disappeared. I opened my eyes.

"Did you hear it?" he asked, enthusiastically.

"I'm not sure. There was something, but it was like a ringing, not a song."

Skyen's eyes lit up. "That is how it starts, so soon you will hear their song. It just takes time," he told me with a smile. Excitedly, he bent his head down towards me.

I stood still, not knowing what to do as his gaze connected with mine and lingered there. For an endless moment I thought he would kiss me, but then he turned away and gazed out at the ocean. I breathed out softly. "I hope I will swim there one day," I commented with a slight wistfulness in my voice.

"I think you will," he said, smiling at me. "And I will swim with you. But now I want to take you to the Blue Forest."

"Cool. I thought it was all water here."

"Not all," he replied. "I think you will like it."

Chapter 14

I slipped my hand inside Skyen's and we headed northwards. The walkways were so numerous that I imagined I would get lost wandering them alone. We passed buildings and so many people, and I lost track of where I was, idly following and dreamily taking in everything I saw.

"I never met anyone like you," my companion said out of the blue, squeezing my hand.

I giggled self-consciously. "Ah, me and my red hair!"

"No, you, just you. There is something and I don't know what it is..."

"Is that a compliment?" I asked, laughing again.

"Yes!" he insisted. "But I cannot seem to find the words I want to say. I hope my actions speak louder."

"They do," I added, unable to stop myself from grinning. But your face says more, I thought, noticing how his eyes lit up. They always seemed to do that in my presence.

As we walked, I remembered that day on the beach when I struggled against my invisible attackers, thinking it was the end, and then seeing his eyes in the darkness, realising I was not alone. I wondered if that was how he felt, that he was no longer alone. I peeked at him and a feeling of calm washed over me. I never would be alone anymore, I thought, and then giggled at myself and my silly romantic imaginings, which I had never realised I was capable of.

"What's so funny?" asked Skyen.

"Nothing, just my own crazy thoughts," I confided.

"Can you tell me them?"

"No!" I blurted out.

"Why?"

"Because you would laugh at me!"

"I promise I wouldn't, far from it," he insisted, looking confused. "You're an enigma."

"Why, thank you," I said. "I was thinking about you."

His smile broadened. "Yes, and how so?"

"I can't tell you..."

"Ah, why must you tease me?"

"Because I can," I replied, laughing. "Oh," I gasped as I turned to see tall trees of the brightest blue appeared before my eyes. Dropping Skyen's hand, I walked forwards and rested my fingers on the rough bark.

"Now it is my turn to laugh!" he joked as my invisible second jaw hit the floor.

I stopped dead. "They weren't there before," I said, pointing, "the trees. They weren't."

"I know. This is the Blue Glade. These trees are wrapped in magic – the magic of the dome."

"Magic?" I asked, turning the word over in my mind. "The mist is thicker here," I added as we stepped between the thick trunks.

Skyen nodded. "Yes, this is the place where it originates."

"I thought it came from the sea..."

"The sea, too, some, but most of it comes from here. It is pure magic."

"How?"

"That's a question for the Balaenoptera," said Skyen. "It is beyond my knowledge."

Gazing up, I could not see where the tips of the branches ended. They seemed to travel up forever, stretching and twisting, the leaves trembling in the breeze and the tops blurring in the mist.

"Do you like it here?" he asked.

"I love it," I gasped, glancing at him. "But, what..? Where is..." I mumbled, spinning around. The walkway had vanished and we were deep inside the woods. "I don't understand."

"It moves," he replied. "I did not want to bring you here before, until you were more used to our city and our ways. It seems that we are deep in the forest, but we are only on the edge of it. If you step this way behind me you will be back on the walkway."

"How is it possible?"

"It is the Blue Glade," Skyen stated, as if that explained everything. "Let's walk. I find this place so restful."

"Will it change again?"

"No, this is as it is."

"Good," I replied, rolling my eyes. "That makes me feel much better."

I stepped a little way ahead, brushing the blue bark with the tips of my fingers. It felt a little warm and seemed to vibrate softly beneath my touch. There was an overwhelming scent here that I did not recognise. Glancing down, I noticed for the first time that the grass was blue. A thought struck me and I slipped my feet out of my sandals. The blades were soft and dry beneath my feet, but they seemed to tickle in an odd way. Giggling, I picked up my footwear and stepped forward.

Skyen watched me, clearly amused. "It tickles, yes?"

"Yeah!" I laughed, turning. "You knew and didn't tell me."

"Of course. It is for you to discover," Skyen replied, taking my hand, "just as you are for me to discover."

Blushing, I looked away, unable to meet his eyes. I could feel them burning into the side of my face and I bit my lip, feeling nervous.

"I make you blush a lot," he remarked.

"Yes," I mumbled, still not looking, "so please stop."

"Do you really want me to?"

I giggled and turned. "No, and you know it!"

Skyen laughed loudly and gazed up at the trees. "You know they speak to one another."

"The trees? No!"

"They do. If you listen, you can hear the rustling of the leaves. They open like hands, don't you think? I imagine them as hands, but they speak. I am sure of it."

"Like the whales sing?" I replied.

He nodded.

"But I can't hear either of them," I answered, laughing again.

"But you will. I am sure of it."

We walked slowly between the trees, listening to the various sounds that broke the quiet. There was no birdsong. I imagined Skyen could hear the whales even here as he was so attuned to them. Suddenly I missed the cheerful chirping of birds. It was strange that fish swam through the air instead of them. I wondered what the blackbird in the hospital garden would think of that, and I smiled to myself.

Reality did not seem to intrude here. My own reality seemed the extraordinary one. This place was beginning to feel like home, and that terrified and excited me in equal measure. As I walked with the young man beside me, I tried to imagine my life here and wondered what it would be truly like. If I never returned home, would I miss it? That place seemed so very far away, so long ago, swept away in a dream that I once imagined. Here I was in a forest of blue and it seemed normal, and I was on the adventure of my life.

"Let's sit here," Skyen suggested as the trees parted to reveal a small, circular clearing with tiny flowers dotted all around.

Nodding, I dropped my sandals and sat down on the soft grass, smoothing down my dress and stretching out my legs. I watched my toes wriggle in the warm air.

"Do you know that..." Skyen began and then stopped.

I looked at him and his gaze overpowered me. Turning away, I spread my fingers wide over the grass and pulled them through the long, soft blades.

"Why can't you look at me?" he asked.

The words lingered in the air longer than the sounds and I wondered this fact myself. As I turned my head, Skyen leaned forward and his warm lips found mine. I felt his hands encircle my waist as my own shifted towards his, and we seemed to curve together, my movements mirroring his. Feeling as though I were falling backwards, I closed my eyes and surrendered to the moment.

Chapter 15

The next few weeks passed as quickly as the previous ones, but I found myself thinking more about my home, my real one, and whether I should go back. I wondered if it would be possible to go and then return once more, but I had not asked Sophia. I imagined she was the only one who knew. If I did go home and found myself unable to return, well, I was not sure what I would do.

I did not want to lose Skyen or my new life here, which seemed kind of magical to me, and yet I felt my heart pulling towards the people I had left behind. My thoughts oft returned to Michael and my grandfather, in particular, and I imagined them doing their regular day-to-day things; nothing would have changed much, except for me not being in their lives. I pondered whether they missed me or if they were sad. I wondered what they had thought when my hospital bed was found to be empty. Then I imagined the police looking for me and the missing person report on the news.

As my heart raced, I pushed the thoughts from my mind. These darkest ideas always filled me with terror and left me worrying about the suffering that I might be causing my family and friends at home. I hoped they were well, but I knew I would have left a hole in their lives.

If only I could click my shoes together like Dorothy and go home just for a while, and then come back again. I would be able to tell my family that I was fine and there was nothing to fear or worry about.

But was that really possible? How much power did the crystal have? Could it take me back and then here again?

Getting up from my bed, I walked to the closet and rummaged through the heap of clothes at the bottom. Picking up my purple hooded top, I brought it up to my face and breathed it in. The scent of the familiar, though faded, remained; the smell of home and everything I knew before. I swallowed hard and put the top down again. Sweeping my hands underneath the clothes, I felt for the pocket in my black tracksuit bottoms until I came across something cold and hard. Feeling the familiar tremor in my hands that I remembered from the past, I crept slowly back to the bed.

The crystal glimmered in my palms, reflecting back the tiny lights all around the room. The blue mist at the very centre appeared to brighten until it glowed. *So radiant.* I lost my gaze within the perfect glass edges, dreaming of my home, remembering pictures that rushed through my mind like the evening tide. These things were gone now, but part of me wanted them back. So torn was I.

Taking a deep breath, I rested the crystal on the bed beside me. For some reason I felt that it knew me, as though the power inside could read my thoughts. If only it could guide me too. I had so many questions, but no one to answer them, and my prior life was one that I had to keep secret, even from the person closest to me.

A knock upon the wall outside woke me from my reverie. *Skyen!* Rising, I walked barefoot to the doorway where the blue mist faded away to nothing as the tips of my fingers touched it, reminding me of falling rain.

Hello," greeted a slim, tall girl, whose long hair was decorated with flowers. Her skin looked even paler today and her beautiful eyes seemed troubled.

"Yava?" I said in surprise, thinking how unusual the scene was. She had never come to my room before. "Is something wrong?"

She stared back at me sadly and nodded slowly. I stepped aside to make way for her. "Come in and tell me what's happened."

The girl nodded again and entered my room. She walked into the middle, stopped and turned to face me. I noticed that her hands were clasped together tightly and sensed that something bad had happened. "Sit down," I urged her. "Do you want a drink or something?"

Yava shook her head. "No. And no..."

"What is it? You can tell me," I said softly. "I know we don't know each other well, but if I can help in any way..?"

"You can't help me," she replied, her eyes darting around the cabin. "No one can."

I looked down at her hands, which she twisted. Yava was looking everywhere but at my face, unable to meet my gaze, it seemed. I stopped staring and glanced away myself. "Please sit down. Tell me what's wrong, or if you want I can find Skyen's sister if..."

"No!" said Yava, raising her voice. "I came here to speak with you."

I nodded, deciding to just hear her out.

"I hate you," she spat, brushing fresh tears away from her cheeks.

Shocked, I took a step backwards and felt a slight chill in the air. Frowning, I smoothed down my dress almost automatically as if my hands needed to do something. I had no idea what to say, so nothing passed my lips. Glancing at the doorway, I wondered if it would be wisest to leave the room.

"Nothing has been the same since the day you arrived here," Yava continued. "Everything changed and it is because of you."

"I don't understand," I answered, taking a step closer to the door. "What did I do to you?"

Yava's expression changed and I saw a darkness surge forth in her tear-filled eyes. "You! He changed. We were friends since childhood and he has changed. He doesn't even see that I exist anymore..."

"Oh," I gasped as realisation swept over me. "You mean Skyen?"

"Of course I mean him," she shouted, her hands shaking and turning into clenched fists by her sides. "You destroyed everything between us."

"I didn't know there was anything between you..."

"There wasn't," she sighed, "yet! And now there can never be because of you! I saw you together. I saw! You, in his arms! I cannot forget it. I have been stuck with that picture in my mind every day."

I slumped down in the chair as if the air had been sucked out of my body. "I'm sorry," I muttered, lost for words. There was nothing I could say. The pain in her eyes was clear for anyone to see and there was nothing I could do about it. Rubbing my forehead, I gazed down at my feet. Skyen had never spoken of Yava in any terms except friendship. He just saw her as his sister's friend, I was certain of it.

"What is this?"

I looked up to see that Yava had her back to me and was holding something in her right fist. Glancing at the bed and seeing nothing there upon the blanket, the cold hand of fear tugged at my heart. Standing, I felt my entire body tremble.

"Is it yours?" the girl asked, spinning round and holding up the sparkling crystal between her fingers.

"Yes," I mumbled, my eyes widening.

"It is spellbinding. How could it be yours? It looks very valuable."

"It is mine," I repeated. "Please give it to me."

I held out my hand, but Yava scowled at me and then she laughed. "Did you steal this?" she demanded to know. "It would not surprise me if someone like you stole it. You know that taking something without permission goes against our code here?"

"It belonged to a friend. Please..."

Yava looked at the crystal in her two palms, shuffling it between them. "So you value this?" she questioned.

Frightened by the fierceness in her expression, I did not answer. An icy wind seemed to sweep through the air as I guessed her thoughts. I dared not say yes and wished anyone would enter the room, just anyone. Glancing at the Time Box on the shelf, I realised that Skyen should have been here by now. *The one time he is late...*

"I should take this," the girl said in spite. "Just as you have taken what belongs to me."

"You can't own a person," I replied. "He has free choice." As soon as the words escaped my lips, I regretted them. Yava took a step closer to me, her face misshapen with contempt. She no longer looked beautiful and I guessed that everyone had misjudged her still, calm demeanour.

A dull knock made me turn sharply. It had to be Skyen. He was the only one who could pass through the door without my opening it, because I had given him permission, but I knew he would wait out of politeness and respect for my privacy.

"Jayne?"

"Don't let him in," Yava spat. "Not now."

I considered my options, but it only took me a moment to decide. "Come in!" I shouted.

Skyen walked into the room, but his warm smile dropped immediately as he took in the scene and the anger that was written across my opponent's face. "What is happening here?" he asked.

"Huh, you've never seen what's going on," shouted Yava, "ever!"

"What?" he asked, looking at me, confused. "Jayne, what is she talking about?"

"I can't say," I replied, hoping to soothe things. "Ask her."

Skyen turned. "Yava?"

"You do not care what I think," she answered, redirecting her anger. "You haven't since you brought *her* here."

Skyen frowned. "I do not understand you."

"I don't think you ever did. I have known you since we were this high," Yava said, waving her hand down towards the floor. "And then you forgot about me when she turned up."

"I forgot about you? What are you referring to? We are friends. We will always be," Skyen replied.

Glancing at his face, I realised he did not have the slightest idea how his friend really felt about him, but then I guessed that no one had. "Yava," I began, trying to diffuse the situation, "maybe we should all just sit down and talk about this. We don't need to argue."

The girl recoiled and her anger rose like a flame. "Perfect, so perfect! You're always trying to be so nice, but I know you're not, even if he can't see it. And this? Is this so precious to you?"

I stared at the crystal, which remained in her grip. I nodded.

"Yava, please give it back to her and calm down," said Skyen, moving towards her.

"I should have guessed you would say that," the girl screeched. "Well, she cannot have it!"

Feeling my stomach turn and my legs tremble, I tried to step forward, but I could not. My limbs were welded to the floor. I looked at Skyen, who turned in increments, as if everything had suddenly slowed down. A flash of light came crashing towards me and I realised it was the crystal. Stretching my hands upwards, I tried to reach it.

The room seemed to bend and bow, creaking like the old wooden sides of a ship, and the roar of the sea sounded in my ears. Something shattered on the floor and a million lights blinded me. As sickness filled my stomach, the air became thick and heavy, choking. I felt my body slide, slipping away. Someone shouted my name and then he was gone.

Chapter 16

Jayne awoke with a jolt and spluttered against the tube in her throat blocking her airflow. Opening her eyes, she felt the sting of a drip in her hand. The eager pumping of her heart thumped in her ears yet the flesh around it seemed weak. She squinted against the harsh glare of fluorescent lighting, making out a row of beds and patients opposite; a rough outline, somewhat fuzzy.

Moving her head ever so slightly, Jayne found her neck to be stiff and sore. Her eye sockets ached and the tips of her fingers felt numb. She attempted to move her right foot, but it did not respond; there was no feeling at all. As confusion and panic washed over her, she gasped for breath and coughed once more.

"Nurse!" a male voice shouted. "She's awake!"

A beeper sounded and footsteps pounded across the floor. Everything seemed too loud.

"Jayne?"

"Uh," she mumbled, unable to reply because of the tube.

Carefully, the nurse removed the obstruction and Jayne responded by coughing some more. After checking the patient and the machine, the woman walked away swiftly. Within a few minutes she returned with two doctors and another nurse.

"How are you feeling?" asked the doctor whose name badge said 'A. Brown'.

"Dizzy," Jane replied. She was able to see clearly, so

that was a good sign, she thought.

"Don't try to talk now," said the doctor. "The nurse has telephoned your grandfather. He is on his way here."

Jayne blinked in response and made no effort to speak. All around her, nurses busied themselves and time seemed to drift in a haze while she tried to concentrate on breathing. She flicked her stiff fingers awkwardly, focusing on their movements and trying to move her arms. Her mind felt heavy, as if a fog were weighing it down.

After an endless time her grandfather's face appeared.

"How are you, petal?" he asked.

Jayne tried her best to smile and received a huge grin in response.

"I see you are fine," he said, taking a seat by her bed. "We'll have you up and about in no time."

"How long... sleep?"

"Jayne, you weren't sleeping. You fell back into a coma. The doctors think your body had not recovered properly from the accident and that was the reason why, or that an infection or virus may have attacked part of your brain. They did a lot of tests and are not sure yet. I'm just relieved you're awake."

"How long..."

"It has been three months, but the doctor believes your condition is stable now."

"Can I go back?" asked Jayne, feeling disorientated.

The old man shook his head. "No, they don't think so. You won't go back into a coma. Nothing is one hundred per cent sure, but, no, I think you will be okay now," he added, taking her hand in his.

Jayne smiled. While happy to see a familiar, dear face, her mind was hazy and no thoughts were clear. All she felt was a strange sense of loss and imbalance, as if she were falling with no one to catch her.

Chapter 17

"Her name is Sophia Ambry," Jayne gushed. "She's about fifty-ish, maybe sixty, but I'm guessing as I only met her once. I've no idea where she lives."

"So, how will I find her?" Michael asked.

"I don't know, but please try, for me. I really have to talk to her."

"Okay, if it means that much to you. I'll start with the internet and her name."

"And please, if you find her, can you give her this note from me? Tell her I was in another coma and I'm still in the hospital, or I would have visited her myself."

"Alright," he said, taking the folded piece of paper. "Don't worry, just rest. I won't ask what it's about. I'm guessing it's something crazy."

Jayne smiled. "Thanks, Michael. You're such a good friend."

"I know," he said, "the best. Now sleep and I'll visit you again soon."

"You better," Jayne said, winking. "See you."

"Bye."

Waving, Michael wandered down the ward and out of the heavy doors. Once outside, he leaned against the wall and took a deep breath. His friend's eccentric imaginings troubled him. It had been a few weeks now and Jayne was still talking about this make-believe world beneath the sea as if it really existed.

When he had feared his friend might never wake, Michael had done a lot of reading on the internet about brain trauma and comas, and now she was back he could not have been happier, but some of the things she said were worrying. He guessed it was her mind in recovery, trying to distinguish reality from fiction. Glancing around, he took the piece of paper out of his jean pocket and unfolded it. He cursed under his breath as he read the words.

Dear Sophia,

I'm sorry to bother you, but I need your help. I used the crystal and I went to Entyre. You must know where I mean. I think you went there too. I came back, but it wasn't by choice. I want to return. There is someone there who means everything to me. I feel like my old self there. I can walk, and I'm healthy and strong. I must go back.

Please help me. I am in the hospital. I was in another coma for three months. I feel weak and like a part of me is missing. My friend thinks I am imagining everything and the doctor says I caught a virus, which affected my brain. I'm so confused. Am I going crazy? Please visit me. Please tell me that I am not going mad and that it was really real. You're the only one who can help me.

With warm wishes,
Jayne

Someone there who means everything? The piece of paper screwed itself up in Michael's grip as he winced under the weight of the words. Not only was his friend imagining some place that did not exist, but she was also missing someone who lived in it. He had to help her stop thinking such ridiculous thoughts, but how?

He wondered whether to speak to one of her doctors about it. Perhaps they would have a solution.

For now, Michael refused to go along with Jayne's fantasies. If he played up to them, it would only take her longer to recover. As he walked along the corridor to the exit, he tossed the note in the nearest bin. He would tell Jayne that he could not find Sophia.

Chapter 18

"Did you find her?" asked Jayne, as soon as Michael reached her bed two days later.

"No."

Jayne's face fell. "Oh."

"But I tried," he lied. "I did a search for her name on the internet and I rang the Post Office, but I couldn't find anything."

"Maybe you could contact a charity?" Jayne suggested, hopefully. "There are national ones that find people."

"I think that's only if you're related to the person and have proof."

"How about the library? They have records."

"I don't think..."

Jayne bit her lip and replied, undaunted, "Well, maybe she will visit me again, like she did that one time."

Michael sat down in the chair by the bed. "Perhaps it would be better to just stop thinking about it."

"But it's all I think about..."

"You can't mean the same old story..."

"But it isn't a story," Jayne argued. "It really happened to me. I was there and I could walk, and I was strong, just as I was before the accident. I think that's why I was in a coma, because half of me wasn't here... the strongest part was somewhere else."

"I don't want to hurt you, but have you heard yourself? You're talking crazy stuff..."

"I'm not insane, Michael."

"What you're saying is. I don't mean you are. I was reading about brain injuries and doctors believe the mind can invent things while the body is healing itself. They say that when patients wake up from a coma, some can't always tell reality from..."

"I know what you're saying, but you're wrong. Why won't you listen to me?"

He sighed. "Because what you're saying is impossible."

"That doesn't mean it didn't happen. I thought you were my friend."

"I am, but I think you're not well... yet. I think maybe you should talk to the doctor about your, erm, beliefs. Maybe he'll know why..."

"Michael, I know what happened."

"Can you prove it to me?" he asked.

Jayne scowled. "No. How can I? Not unless you go there yourself."

"Yeah, let's all go time travelling. Cool. Let me know when it's convenient."

"Michael! Look, maybe you should just go home," Jayne said with tears in her eyes. "I'm not in the mood to talk anymore."

The young man stood up. "Fine. I'll come back when you're in a better mood and not talking crazy shit."

Jayne watched her friend stalk off without a backward glance. When he was gone, she brushed the hair back from her face and twisted her hands in her lap, feeling hurt and frustrated. She knew that she was not making it up. However fantastic it sounded, she was sure that she did visit a city beneath the sea. It existed.

But what if Michael is right? What if my imagination invented it all?

Jayne remembered Sophia visiting her before, so that was proof that it must have happened. But what if she had still been ill? Had her mind been playing tricks on her all this time, even back then, due to her injuries?

Jayne stared up at the ceiling. There were so many 'buts' to everything. None of the scenarios that her mind conjured up made total sense. It all seemed so real, but had it really been just a lucid dream? Leaning back against the pillow, she closed her eyes, but all she could see was blue.

Chapter 19

Over the next few weeks Jayne concentrated on getting better. The dark mood that she had found herself in grew steadily lighter and she pushed her memories of the blue city to the back of her mind, dismissing them as dreams, which would gradually fade with time. That was her hope, for while she was sleeping her mind wove images of the sea, accompanied by the echo of the whales and a tall man whose hair was the colour of the darkest waves. He was always there, not far away it seemed, thus was the lucidity of her sleeping life.

While awake, Jayne focused on the here and now. Her doctor informed her the tests proved his theory that the coma had been caused by an infection and the confusion she experienced was due to its impact on her brain, accompanied by the earlier trauma caused by the accident. He seemed positive that her haziness and forgetfulness would pass, and that the distinction between what was real and unreal would become clearer.

Jayne was allowed to move back home to stay with her grandfather, where Michael and Angela came to visit her often. Her grandfather drove her to her physiotherapy sessions and other appointments at the hospital, and Michael always seemed to be there when she needed someone to talk to about her deepest fears, which were always about the future. It scared her that she would never be able to do all of the things she used to take for granted. Being unable to walk was the biggest mental block for her, but she was fighting it. Her willpower became her friend, and she found a new freedom in being at home, and being able to get out and about in her wheelchair.

Following months of physiotherapy, Jayne's upper body had become strong and she felt able to participate in sports, which she found fun, to her surprise. Being around other women who had overcome similar disabilities, she found their determination to be fit and happy inspired her to push her own boundaries. She also made new friends. Far from feeling that her life was over, Jayne realised that it was simply re-beginning in a different format. As her grandfather always liked to remind her, as one door closes another opens.

Jayne signed up for evening school and took up her studies again, hoping to complete her exams and go on to college. Her aim was to find a part-time job as well to help out her grandfather, or at least to lessen her dependence on him.

As the seasons changed, she never again mentioned the months she spent in the city beneath the sea. With time, she hoped the memories would begin to fade. It was only when she slept that her mind wandered back into the blue.

And so it was that one day, about a year after waking from her second coma, Jayne was heading to the library with Michael. It was a fresh spring morning and the sun cast a soft glow, its light picking out the delicate blossom on the trees. Jayne loved this time of year as she could feel a new beginning in the air and the time for warm clothes appeared to be leaving. As they approached the doors of the building, Michael ran ahead. "I'll open it," he said.

"I wish they would get electric ones. They're so far behind the times," Jayne called out. "How am I supposed to get in without you?"

"I guess you could keep ramming the glass until you annoy them enough to answer."

"I'm thinking about it," Jayne replied with a giggle as she wheeled through the open door. "Thanks."

"I'm heading to the horror section," said Michael. "Catch you in a bit."

"Okay," Jayne replied, heading towards the children's section. For some reason she had been reading a lot of books meant for kids since her accident. She guessed it was escapism of some kind. Either that or she had regressed somehow. Stopping her chair, Jayne read the titles of the books as high as she could manage. She had no idea what was on the fourth shelf up. It would remain a mystery, she thought, smiling.

Scanning the spines, she stopped at *Fantastic Mr Fox* and pulled it out, followed by a collection of Hans Christian Andersen's tales. Jayne had checked the book out so many times and always meant to buy a copy. Every month she would read *The Little Mermaid*, which she connected with on some subconscious level.

"That'll do for this week," she told herself, before making her way back towards the front of the library. As she neared the main desk, she stopped abruptly. A leaflet on the table caught her attention. Picking it up, she read the words 'Paintings of The Sea Inside by Sophia Ambry' as the paper shook between her fingers. "Oh, God," she gasped, almost dropping it.

"Are you alright?" asked the librarian.

"Yes, I'm fine," Jayne replied, turning her chair around. She made her way across the library as quickly as she could to where she knew the horror section to be. Michael was sitting on the floor with a book open on his lap and another one beside him.

"What's wrong?" he asked, looking up. "You look like you've seen a ghost."

"Well, I'd be in the right section then," Jayne replied, pushing towards him. "Look what I found. It's her!"

"Who?" Michael asked. Jumping up, he closed the space between them. "Let me see."

"It's her, Sophia Ambry! She paints!"

Michael felt a twist in his stomach as he read the leaflet. "Are you sure?" he asked, knowing full well that it was.

"Yes, I recognised her, and the name fits," Jayne replied with a big smile. "So will you..."

"You're not going to see her, are you?"

"Okay, Mr Grumpy, stop! You don't have to come. I know what you think about all this."

Michael passed the leaflet back to her. "I thought you'd given up on this fantasy. The doctor said it was caused by you being ill, and you haven't even mentioned it since then."

Jayne tutted loudly. "Yeah, dippy, that's because I knew what you'd say if I did, but this is a sign. It's fate. I have to speak to her. It will be good closure for me. Then I can file away the whole experience."

"No, I know you. You're kidding me. You still believe..."

"I just want to know the truth about everything, that's all. As in I want to ask her about the time she visited the hospital. She's an artist. For all I know, I may have just seen one of these leaflets before or her picture somewhere and then just imagined she visited me. Do you get me?"

Michael shrugged. "Well, that makes sense, I guess, and it might help you to see why you imagined it all."

Jayne grinned. "See, I'm right, as always."

"I dunno about that," the guy replied, bending down to scoop up his books. "Anyway, I'm getting these two. When does it say the exhibition is?"

"Next week," Jayne replied.

"Okay, so I'll come with you. Is it local?"

"I can't wait that long. She has a website where people can buy her paintings. I'm going to contact her."

"But..."

"No buts, Michael," Jayne replied. "Also, if she has a website, that means she is on the internet, but you said you couldn't find her."

He glanced away, looking flustered. "Erm, I, erm..."

"You didn't look, did you?" she demanded, scowling.

"Erm, no, I didn't. Look, I was worried about you."

"It's okay," Jayne replied. "I get it. You were doing it 'cos you thought I was crazy, yeah?"

He shifted from one foot to the other. "I'm sorry."

"You're forgiven as I've no idea what to think anymore, and I probably would have done the same." She paused as an idea entered her head. "Don't tell me you read that note I gave you for Sophia?" she asked, to which he blushed again. "Michael! You..."

The lad sprinted towards the librarian's desk, gripping his books under his arm. It was the only way to avoid his friend's fury, which he'd witnessed a few times before and was in no hurry to see again.

"Damn it," Jayne muttered, as she pushed her chair forwards. She imagined Michael reading the words she had written in the note and squirmed, embarrassed to the tips of her toes.

Chapter 20

"Thank you for seeing me," said Jayne when the door to the ivy-covered, old brick house opened.

"My pleasure," replied Sophia, but then a look of disappointment clouded her face. "I'm afraid your chair is too wide to come through here. I'm sorry. What can I do?"

"It's okay, it happens all the time. He can help me. Sophia, this is my friend, Michael."

"Good day, young man. If you're sure you can manage..."

"Do it all the time," he replied. "I'll carry Jayne inside. Just lead the way. Then I'll come back and fold the chair, and leave it in the hallway, if that's okay."

"Yes, that's fine," answered the woman, pushing a strand of grey hair behind her ear. "It must be a constant problem. Doorways are so small."

"You'd be surprised," Jayne replied. "Public transport is a nightmare and going to the cinema, well, it seems I'm a fire hazard a lot of the time!"

"Dear me," Sophia remarked, shaking her head, "and in this day and age too. Come this way into the lounge, my favourite room. I've made a pot of tea and there are some biscuits there on the table. Sit down wherever is comfortable. If you're hungry, I can make you a sandwich."

She led the way into a spacious room, painted aquamarine. The wooden furniture was light brown - probably beech, guessed Jayne - but the furnishings and fabric of the two sofas were all blue. She instantly thought of the mist because it was the exact same shade. Glancing up at her host, she realised that she must not have forgotten her own adventure.

"So, how have you been?" asked Sophia once they were all seated.

"Okay," Jayne replied. "I've been getting better and stronger all the time. I was very down to begin with, but with the help of Michael and my grandfather, I'm improving. I feel happier."

Sophia smiled warmly. "Good, good, I am glad to hear this."

"She has been playing sports and is back at college," Michael chipped in. "We're very proud of her."

"And how are you?" asked Jayne.

"Well, I'm still here," replied Sophia. "At my age, every new day is a blessing. Here, please have some tea."

Jayne took the cup, warming her hands around it. Glancing around the room, she caught sight of a series of three paintings. The canvases were huge, but it was the scenes within that caught her eye: the azure sea, some dolphins, a dome under the ocean, a city filled with light, and a single whale in the last. He rose up from the ground, towering over a slight-figured girl with long blonde hair, behind which was a trail of steps leading upwards.

"You remember, no?" asked Sophia, following her line of sight.

Jayne swallowed. "Yes. They are beautiful."

"They are my memories," the woman added, wistfully.

Michael gazed at the pictures with a confused expression on his face. "These remind me of the things in the stories you kept telling me about."

Jayne bit her lip and nodded.

"But how?" he asked, looking lost for words.

"You do not believe her then?" asked Sophia.

Jayne looked up. "How did you guess?"

"It's written all over his face. It is true, Michael, I am afraid. I was there."

The young man shook his head, looking bewildered. "They are just pictures."

"Indeed," muttered Sophia. "So, Jayne, why did you want to see me so urgently?"

"I-I want to go back," Jayne replied. "I need to..."

"But you left?"

Jayne shook her head. "I didn't choose to. The crystal broke, but I didn't break it, and then I found myself in the hospital again."

"Oh, my dear..."

"I was in Entyre for three months, but the doctors told me I'd spent the same length of time in a coma. They said I imagined everything because of an infection or virus or something that affected my brain. So, I began to doubt myself. I had therapy and I've been rebuilding my life, but..."

Sophia leaned forward. "But what?"

"I have to go back. I met... I miss Entyre. Part of me feels that I belong here, but a bigger part of me knows I *should* be there, and it's getting worse. I dream about the city every night; every single night. It's like I'm really there, but then I wake up."

"I have those dreams too," Sophia said softly.

"So you get me..."

"Don't you realise you're imagining it all?" asked Michael. "You were in a coma! I read that the brain can trick you into thinking things are real when they're not."

"No, I did not imagine it. We've spoken about this so much, Michael. I thought you got it by now?"

"How can I? It makes no sense. And, lady, with all due respect, you're just adding to the problem. You're making her think that what she imagines is true," said Michael, his voice rising.

"Michael, that's rude," said Jayne. "I'm sorry, Sophia."

"It is quite alright," the woman answered, taking a sip of her tea. "No one believed me either. When I came back, I was also in a coma."

"See," Michael cried out, "that's all it is. Make believe!"

Jayne glanced at her friend with a weary look on her face. "Again, I'm sorry, Sophia. Michael, it is true."

"Whatever," he mumbled. "I thought you were getting better."

Jayne breathed out loudly and rubbed the side of her head in frustration. "Sophia, I wanted to ask if you can help me get back."

Michael stood up and strode out of the room. The front door slammed.

"He thinks I'm making it all up and that it might be a sign that I have some illness," explained Jayne wearily.

The older woman smiled. "It's fine, dear. I've heard it all before. Everyone thought I was talking like a lunatic. But I think the boy cares about you deeply."

Jayne frowned. "Michael? No, we've been friends since we were little."

"Well, that's what my eyes tell me. But, never mind, tell me, how was it there?"

"Wonderful," Jayne remarked, her eyes glazing over. "I could walk. I felt whole again and light. I've never felt so weightless and free, and every day was like waking up all over again, not knowing what would happen next. The strange thing is that I began to feel at home, but I also felt guilty. I missed my family and friends. Part of me wanted to leave, but I knew that if I did, I'd want to go back. The city is like nothing on Earth and the whales..."

"I miss their song," said Sophia, gazing at the paintings. "When I wake up every morning I expect to hear them, but everything is silent."

"I never got to hear them properly. I met someone and I miss him. It has been a long time now, but I still think about him. Tried to forget, but I can't," Jayne admitted. "I think there will always be something missing in me if I stay here."

"So, what happened for the crystal to break?"

"It was smashed by a girl who was jealous of us."

Sophia looked down at her tea cup. "I see."

"I didn't even get to say goodbye," Jayne mumbled, blinking back tears that threatened to spill over.

"And you would like my help?"

"Yes, if you can. You were the one who gave me the crystal. I wondered if you had another or knew where I could find one."

Sophia gazed at her hands, which she turned in her lap. The fingertips trembled slightly. "You might not be able to go back."

"But..."

"But I do have more crystals."

Chapter 21

Jayne leaned forward with tears of joy in her eyes. "Thank goodness. I knew you could help me. But where did they come from? How did you get them? Please tell me."

"Hush now," Sophia replied, setting down her cup and leaning back. "I will tell you my story, as I remember it. My grandmother, Ida, left me the crystals in her will. She often told me a story about her sister when I was a child. First of all, I thought it was something she made up. Later, I discovered otherwise.

"The two sisters loved to play together, acting out stories they invented, pretending to be other people. The younger, wilder Rose found the crystals in their grandparent's attic in a box belonging to their grandmother, who had recently passed away. The sisters kept them as their precious secret, and would take them out and try to see what was inside – as you know, you can see... yes, you remember.

"One winter there was an outbreak of influenza and Rose became very, very ill. There was nothing the doctors could do. The girl grew weaker by the day. Ida was not allowed to hug her sister in case she caught the illness. She was only allowed to stand in the doorway and speak briefly. Finally, the doctors told her parents that Rose would soon die. It was to be a matter of days. The family was grief-stricken, as you can imagine, but especially Ida.

"Against her parents' wishes, Ida snuck into Rose's

room that night, taking with her a handful of the precious crystals, knowing their wonder would cheer her sister. They could lose themselves in imagining all kinds of creatures living in the centre of the blue mist.

"Of course, we both know their imaginings were not just that," continued Sophia with a warm smile. "Rose would not allow her sister to come close to her, afraid she would get sick, so Ida placed one of the crystals into her hands and stood back by the window, watching Rose's face light up at the beauty within.

"Ida told me she stayed with her sister like that for an hour. Rose could not lift her head from the pillow, but her expression was one of simple happiness and gratitude, lost as she was in the heart of the crystal. At some point, Rose thanked Ida, and told her how much she loved her and would miss her. Ida began to cry, which made her sister weep also.

"In that moment a bright light drenched everything, blinding Ida and making her turn to the window. With the world outside so dark, she opened her eyes to see a reflection in the dim glass. Her sister vanished before her eyes, but only for the briefest second. Then the light faded. Ida ran over to Rose, only to find her worst fear a reality. Her sister breathed no more. Through her tears, Ida realised the crystal was gone and there was a peaceful smile on the face of Rose.

"Ida searched everywhere for the crystal, but it was never found. In her heart she knew that her beloved sister was elsewhere for she had seen her disappear, if only for a moment. Although she was sad, the belief that Rose was alive somewhere else kept her strong. She never told anyone, fearing they would think her mad with grief, but she kept the crystals.

"I do not know if my grandmother ever used them herself, but when they were passed down to me they numbered eight. I have often hoped that Ida did in fact follow her sister and find her somewhere."

Jayne sighed. "That's a beautiful story. Her tears took her away, just like me. I was crying the first time."

"As was I," remembered Sophia. "It seems a lifetime ago."

"But why do you say it might not be possible for me to go back?"

"Because I wanted to return and I could not."

Chapter 22

"Why did you leave?" Jayne asked.

Sophia glanced down. "It was not out of choice, as with you. It was an accident. I had a family there. A husband and a young child..."

Jayne bit her lip. "I'm so sorry, I didn't know..."

"How could you? We have never talked so long. He was a kind, good man. I spent twelve happy years in Entyre. Then one awful day, when my child was nine, and as curious as children often are, he searched through my things in the room I shared with my husband inside our cabin. I believe that is what happened. I think he was only curious; it was not his fault. My son found the crystal, but when I walked into the room and asked him what he was holding behind his back, he tried to run from fright and dropped it."

"Oh, my God," Jayne gasped, covering her mouth with her hand.

"And I awoke back here," Sophia continued with barely a break in her sentences. "So, I too, wanted to return. I wanted nothing more. I was told, like you, that I had been in a coma for twelve years, but I knew where I had been. My body had borne a child. There was no denying that. After a long, dark time in which I thought the grief would kill me, I thought about returning."

"But you didn't."

"Well..."

"I am sorry for what happened to you, but I have to go back. Please help me," Jayne pleaded.

Sophia shook her head slowly. "I don't know that I can. How long has it been?"

"A year and..."

"A year is a long time. I think the two times run parallel, but I do not understand how. The power is in the crystal, but if I try to help you, I might only prolong your suffering."

"How?"

"It takes a toll on the body," Sophia explained. "How old do you think I am?"

Jayne gazed at her face. "Fifty-five. Sixty at the most?"

"I am forty-three."

Jayne raised her hand to her lips.

"I aged. When I awoke from the coma it took a long time for me to recover. I had a lot of physiotherapy and I was in the hospital for some time. My left-hand side is still weaker. Yes, I was afraid to go back to Entyre, but in the end I had to. I had a husband and a child there. I had no choice."

"What happened?"

Sophia took a deep breath. "Many things, but what really matters is that I did not go back to the place I left. It had changed. Time had moved on without me."

"I don't mind if he is older. I don't..."

"I'm not talking about a few years. Everyone I had known was... was gone. They had all died. My husband... my child..."

Sophia stopped talking for a moment. "I had nothing left. Devastated, I saw no use in living at all and I smashed the crystal myself. It had brought me nothing but despair. Again, I awoke from a coma here. Though the period of time that had passed was small, I was weaker and I had to heal myself yet again. I am not the same person I was. I do not wish this same fate for you."

Jayne was silent as she took in the words. She could not imagine losing a husband and a child. Her heart went out to the woman sitting opposite, who had been through so much, and here she was, asking questions and making her remember what had hurt her most. "I'm sorry," she said. "I am being selfish. I should not be asking you."

"It is not your fault."

"But you're still here. You got through it," said Jayne, trying to lift the mood. "And you're a great painter."

Sophia smiled wanly. "Yes, I am here, but it has been many years. I was very young, like you, when it all happened. When I returned that second time, I did not want to live, as I told you. I kept myself away from people for a long time and I think it was my painting that saved me. It gave me purpose and I was driven to depict all the things I had seen. Gradually, I recovered, but it took so long. Then one day it was like I could see the sun shining once again. I didn't think I ever would. I sold one painting to an art gallery and it led to more, and I have been able to make a living from that. But I never stopped dreaming about Entyre."

"The paintings are so like…"

"Yes, thank you, but, Jayne, I feel responsible for the position you are in," said Sophia. "When I read about your story in the newspaper, you reminded me of myself. I didn't know if you would wake, but I decided that if you did, I would visit you and offer you a new life, somewhere else. At the time, the doctors did not expect you to recover, and I thought of Rose. I knew your body could be whole and healthy in that other place. You would have a second chance at a full life. I am sorry it has brought you suffering. Perhaps the power in the crystal is dark after all."

"But I'm okay," Jayne replied, leaning forward to touch Sophia's hand. "I'm grateful to you. Life seemed bleak to me and you only tried to help. I was happy in Entyre and free of pain. I found myself. Maybe I grew up," she added with a slight laugh. "Sophia, you gave me hope and I returned a stronger person. I am sure of that."

"So why risk going back?"

Jayne bit her lip and gazed into the old woman's face. "Because I think my destiny lies there."

"I see. And you are determined?"

Jayne nodded.

"What about your family and friends who are here?"

"That is the thing that has been tearing me apart, but I know I want the adventure. I need it. I have spent a year turning it over. I will never be satisfied here and I am willing to take the risk. I only wish that my grandfather would not be alone."

As Sophia gazed into the young girl's innocent green eyes for a few moments, lost memories came flooding back and her decision was made. Slowly, she raised herself to her feet. "Wait here."

Jayne watched the woman disappear from the room. Turning, she took in the paintings of the city beneath the dark depths of the limitless ocean, almost smelling the salty sea as her eyes disappeared into them. If only she could hear the sound of the whales.

She could not imagine the suffering that Sophia must have endured.

"Here," said the old woman upon her return.

Jayne turned slightly to see a small, black velvet bag being held out to her. "There is one inside. I hope you find what you need."

"I hope so, too," Jayne said, taking the gift. "I will never forget you."

Sophia took her seat and poured another cup of tea, her skinny fingers trembling all the while. Jayne closed her hand over the black bag, feeling the tremor of the mysterious object inside. She did not dare to wish for what she wanted the most. Time would provide an answer.

Chapter 23

"I'm going to go to bed now. Good night," Jayne said to her grandfather, leaning forward to hug him.

"Good night, petal," he replied.

Jayne held on tightly, breathing in the scent of her grandfather's jumper, and inhaling a mixture of stale smoke and the scent of wood. He always smelt the same, she thought, not wanting to let go.

It was he who pulled away first. "Is something wrong?" he asked.

"No, I was just thinking that I want to thank you."

"For what?"

"For looking after me, listening, doing everything..."

"But that's my job, love, since your parents passed away. It's my pleasure. Now don't think such silliness and get some sleep. See you in the morning."

"Night, grandpa," said Jayne softly.

Lifting herself into her wheelchair, she regarded at the old man, taking in every detail of his profile. Sitting in his favourite spot, wearing his battered brown-checked slippers, he was happily engrossed in the old, black-and-white Bogart movie, which he'd probably seen numerous times before. Already, he seemed so far away.

How can I leave him?

Swallowing down the putrid guilt rising in her throat, Jayne headed towards her room and went inside. Closing the door, she opened the drawer next to her bed and took out the black velvet bag. Feeling its warmth, she placed it on top of the duvet cover and hauled herself up to lay beside it. "Is this what I really want?" she asked herself.

Pulling the cord that secured the bag, Jayne shook it with her right hand until the shiny contents tumbled out. The sight of the glimmering object brought everything back like the rushing tide. The sea inside shone like a thousand small drops of rain, shaken and glistening. A myriad blues, all interwoven with that enigmatic something deep in the centre.

Picking up the crystal, Jayne stared into the heart of it. The thing unnerved her and she felt it vibrate in her hand as if it were alive. "Do I even want to try?" she asked aloud. Glancing at the door, she thought of her grandfather – what would he do without her? He had no one. She wondered at the person she had become.

Can I really do such an ungrateful thing and leave him? Is my selfish desire to walk stronger than my love for my grandfather, who has always been there for me? And Skyen, is he really more important than my family and friends here? I have no idea if he'll even remember me. Perhaps he will have found someone else.

What if time has moved on, like Sophia warned? What then? I will be alone. I will have given up everything for nothing. But what am I giving up? I want to walk and I want to feel strong, and free, as I was before. Is that too much to want? Am I wrong? Or am I attracted to danger – is that it? Is my need for adventure so strong? Have I changed so much?

Jayne lay back and sighed. She knew the answers to all the questions, but could she do it? Would she be able to live with the guilt?

An idea sprung into her head and she reopened the

drawer beside her bed. Hauling her body closer to the pillows, she sat up and flicked through the numerous items until she found it: the leaflet. Smoothing it out, she placed it on top of one of the pillows. Then, taking out her notepad and a pen, Jayne turned to an empty page and considered what to write.

Dear Grandpa,

First of all, I am sorry, and I want to thank you for getting me through all the dark times since the accident, and all the things you did to try to make me feel like nothing had changed – to make me feel normal. I love you so much and will miss you always. Please don't be sad. I have to go, but I cannot explain and I don't know how to say goodbye. I will not say it because it is too final.

Do you remember when you used to read me stories when I was little, and how I loved 'The Little Mermaid'? She wanted to walk and there was a magical spell, which meant she could, and she found her prince and herself. I am like her, Grandpa. Do you remember the story I told you, about Entyre? I did not imagine this one. It is real. And that is the place I must go. Please don't worry. I will be fine there.

I wish I could take you with me. I know this won't make any sense and you will worry, but please don't. I haven't told any of my friends, not even Michael. I wouldn't know where to begin with him.

I ask only one thing – to contact this lady, Sophia Ambry. See her paintings on the leaflet? Don't you recognise my descriptions of Entyre in them? It is my wish that you meet her. Things will make sense then. She is kind, Grandpa. I know you will like her.

Please keep this a secret, no matter who asks. No one will believe it, but I know you will. You always loved stories about adventure as much as me. I will always be your little petal.

Love, Jayne.

She placed the pad on the pillow with the leaflet underneath it, so that it would not dislodge. Sitting up, she took a long, last look around the room. She had made her decision, at last. It was dark outside and Jayne could discern the glow of the streetlight beyond the window, casting a yellow haze. Never again would she look at it, or anything else in this house or this street, she thought. Looking down at the shimmering piece of glass, she wished a choice did not have to be made. If only she could take everyone with her. If only it were possible.

A tear trickled down Jayne's face and she sighed. Lifting the crystal in her hands, she held it against her chest, waiting, wondering what would come to pass this time. She knew it had worked once. It had never been a dream – it had always been real; as true as the tear that trickled down her cheek and as irrefutable as the fact that her grandfather would now be alone. The thought made her break into sobs, which rocked her body.

A droplet fell and landed on the crystal where it scattered across the surface of blue glass, causing it to shimmer more brightly. As Jayne stared down at it, the object began to blaze in an indigo haze and a ghostly mist began to revolve within. She gasped as the brightness blinded her and in the far distancing she heard the crystal shatter. A burning sensation ripped through her palm and her eyes closed.

Part Two

How could I have doubted myself even once?
It was never a dream.

Chapter 24

A searing, stabbing pain in my hand made me open my eyes with a gasp. I squinted in the bright sunlight, which was as red as blood, embedded in a dark blue sky. "It worked! I remember this," I cried out, standing up. "I'm back!"

Clapping my hands together, I burst out laughing, but then images of my grandfather and Michael flooded my brain and I sobered immediately. It was to be a sweet, but sad homecoming then. I stepped forward, feeling pinpricks in the soles of my feet, but it was a small price to pay. Opening my hand, the pure light of the crystal shone into my face. Around it my palm was bruised. Smiling, I placed the object in the pocket of my loose-fitting trousers.

Rubbing my eyes and feeling as if I had been asleep for a week, I surveyed my surroundings, which seemed familiar, yet distant in memory. I recalled waking here in this exact place amongst these trees that first time a year ago. Everything appeared to be the same. Turning, I thought of Skyen and I had to calm myself. I could not wait to see him again.

I walked in the direction that I remembered through the lush, green swathe of trees, which stretched up high above my head, treading the carpet of red and golden leaves. I gazed down at the contrast they made with my purple and white trainers, and I kicked at them.

There was not a breeze in the air and the sun felt hot. I took off my green hoodie and tied it around my waist, brushing my red hair behind my shoulders in the process. As I stepped forwards, I caught sight of the ghostly blue, slipping between the branches all around me and looking bolder in the path ahead. An uncanny sense of déjà vu drifted over me as I looked into the mist and watched it dissipate.

How could I have doubted myself even once? It was never a dream.

The forest was silent, except for the crunch of crispy leaves beneath the soles of my feet. The air smelt green and the misty trail through the trees beckoned. I followed. After a while, the blue-streaked tree trunks grew further apart and a low hum filled the air. It faded away if I listened too hard and I imagined the trees breathing.

Thinking of Skyen and the city beneath the waves, I felt an ache in the pit of my stomach. Whether it was from fear, anxiety or excitement, I was not sure, but I increased my pace, desiring to reach my destination as soon as possible. Still, I trod carefully, wary that I might fall, even though I recalled that my legs never gave way the first time I was here. Something inside me just did not believe it. After a while I began to run, my heart pumping in my chest, and I felt free again.

I stopped, having reached the point where the trees fused together into a wall of impenetrable wood. Stretching out my fingers, I felt my way along the familiar bark. To my right the blue mist lingered, and I spotted a gap between the forest and the wall of trees; the narrow passageway where I had once walked. I moved forward into the light, charging forwards until the mist became too thick. No longer able to see anything clearly, I slowed down to a walk, remembering with some trepidation what to expect next.

Pressing on, I tried to focus as my eyes grew accustomed to the gloom and then I sensed something stir by my feet. I stumbled as cold fear crept up the back of my neck. The ground appeared to be shifting and I started to run in the dark, trailing my fingers along the wall of bark. Something grabbed at my feet and I sprinted as fast as I could, but I knew what was coming because I had lived through it before. Dread filled me as I surged forward towards the beach, which I sensed was near. The line of bark turned sharply and I gazed out on the ocean. Everything was blue and I felt a pulling sensation in my stomach. I was so close.

Chapter 25

Stepping on to the sand, I looked up at the huge white moon, surrounded as it was by a halo of silver, glowing brightly in the midnight-blue sky. Around me circled the familiar mist that had been my guide so many times, but all I could hear was deathly silence, except for the sombre lap of the surf on the shoreline. My feet sank and sand sprinkled the laces of my trainers.

Slipping on my hooded top, I shivered as the air blew against me, soundless but cold. In the quiet an eerie wind began to howl, far out amongst the dark waves. Then I saw them, the shadows. They darted to and fro around me, but I sensed them more than seeing as they vanished as soon as I tried to focus on them.

I took a deep breath, knowing the terror that lay beneath the sand. Daring myself to look down, I stepped closer to the water's edge, hoping the swimmers of Entyre would be in the sea, still looking out for people to rescue and protect, but I sensed that I was banking on chance. This stark reality and the blind naivety of my plan hit me.

Inevitably, hands gripped at my feet. I hopped and looked down, but there was nothing there. Fingers pulled at my flowing hair, but they were ethereal. As something frigid encircled my throat, I coughed and screamed, my voice lost in the quietude. Terror filled me then, just as it had a year before.

Running towards the sea, despite my fear of it, I bounded straight in until the shivery waves swept up to my knees. I scrutinised the entire length of beach, but there was nothing to see; only the flicker of a shadow that soon lost itself. As the biting wind blew, I held my tangled hair back off my face with one hand to prevent it whipping my cheeks. Behind me the ocean stretched, deep and dark, unfathomable.

Water still frightened me, but it was better than lingering on the sand. I waited, knee deep in the waves that surged. Concentrating hard, I began to count in a bid to suppress the sensation of panic that was fast rising in my chest, willing myself not to scream. In the darkness I heard a high-pitched wail and it was a few endless moments before I realised it was my own voice, swept up upon the air like the caw of a bird.

"Here!"

I spun around against the tumult of the sea and stepped forward. Tasting salt in my mouth, I shouted back, "Hey!"

"Swim out," the man called.

"I can't swim," I cried out, my voice breaking in the wind. "I'm afraid." I walked further out until the water dipped just below my shoulders and I shivered.

In the blue dark I could see a pair of eyes and an image of Skyen flashed through my head.

Is it he?

I blinked against the droplets of water that shot into my face with every crash of a wave. I could not tell whether it was Skyen as the tone of his voice was lost in the chaos. His eyes grew closer and the scenery seemed to fall back in slow motion as the wind wailed.

My words stuck in my throat as his face grew closer,

until I could trace all of its fine lines and the dark blue hair. He stretched out his hand to me, but it was not he. It was a stranger who picked me up and told me to hold my breath before whisking me down into the depths of the sea.

It isn't him.

I closed my eyes as I felt my body being tugged down into the deep; down, down, down into the dark, gripped in a firm hold.

It isn't him.

Time stopped and yet seemed to gush on endlessly. At the very end of my endurance, the arms released me and my legs gave way. My hands felt ground beneath me and I opened my eyes.

"You are in the city of Entyre," said the man, pushing his long, wet hair behind his shoulders. Drops of water clung to his eyelashes as he looked at me intently. "Are you well?"

"Y-yes," I stammered. "I-I've been h-here before."

"You are cold," he said, reaching for a blanket, which he draped around my shoulders. He rubbed my arms briskly in a bid to warm them up. "Don't move."

"I c-came back," I whispered, but the man just stared at me with concern. "Don't talk," he told me.

"But I've been here before. I need to see Skyen."

"Skyen? Do you know his whole name?" the man asked, sitting back on his haunches.

Trembling with cold, I willed my mind to remember. "S-skyen Yij A-arind Lanyajigan," I muttered at last.

The man glanced down and back up at me. Moving forward, he gently took my hand in his and rubbed it. "He is one with the sea," he stated, but the words failed to register. I stared at his face blankly as I felt my body sinking through the floor. I could only picture blackness. The man rubbed my arm delicately. "He died in the Great Battle, as many did. Most of his family passed over."

I looked up, my lips trembling as noise raged in my ears. I could hear nothing anymore.

"He was a hero," the man added before everything went dark.

Chapter 26

In the morning I left the cabin that I had been allocated and walked swiftly down the silent corridor to the steps that would take me to my necessary destination. My body felt hot and sticky from where I had slept in my clothes, and I had not checked my appearance. Feeling lost, I wandered, blind to everything I passed. There was only one place I wanted to go. Nothing else mattered.

I stopped in front of the tall building that resembled the spiral trunk of a tree. A memory popped into my head as I gazed into the doorway, glistening with blue mist. Skyen stood there for a moment, telling me, "This is the Centre of Knowing." Blinking, I pushed him away and walked through the shimmering.

Inside, I was struck by the familiarity of the huge expanse of space. I had been here before, but everything was wrapped up with the memory of Skyen. A vision of him seemed to echo everywhere. Swallowing, I cursed my weakness and made my way across the floor of the building towards the place I needed to go. I have to be stronger. Passing the rows of 'books', I remembered Skyen picking up what looked to be a slice of glass and explaining to me its function. Picturing myself gazing into it with awe, it was with some trepidation that I halted beside the glittering disc on the ground.

"What are you doing?"

I turned to see a tall man with short blue hair staring at me intently. "You cannot go there," he said.

My hands trembled as I brushed my straggly hair back from my face. "I need to see them."

"You wish to speak with the Rulers of the Deep?" the man asked, raising an eyebrow.

I nodded as my bottom lip quivered. Feeling tears at the back of my eyes, I cursed my stupidity in thinking that I could return to the exact same time. Of course, it had always been impossible. Sophia had tried to warn me and I ignored her.

The man's expression flickered to one of concern. "Are you alright, Miss?"

I shook my head, unable to speak.

"Come and sit over here," he suggested, leading me by the arm to a couple of glass-looking chairs. "I am one of the librarians. Now, please explain to me what the issue is."

When I had recovered myself sufficiently, I told him, "I need to speak to the Balaenoptera. I was here once before, but a long time ago, it seems. I journeyed back yesterday, and the people I knew are now dead and I don't know what to do." As I spoke, exhaustion washed over me and I began to sob.

The librarian bent down until his face was on a level with mine. "I think you speak of the flows of time, but this is something of which my knowledge is insufficient. I can make an appointment for you. All citizens are welcome to meet the Balaenoptera. As you are a new arrival, you will have to be greeted anyway. How does tomorrow sound to you?" he asked.

Glancing up, I wiped my tears with the sleeve of my top and nodded with a half smile.

"Come back here in the morning," the man said, kindly. "In the meantime I suggest you return to your cabin and try to relax. You should wash and sleep, and eat something. There is nothing that can be done until tomorrow."

I nodded. "Y-you are right, I know. Thank you."

"It is my pleasure. Can you make your way back?"

"Yes, yes," I mumbled, getting up. "You are kind. Goodbye."

As though in a trance, I wandered across the floor, barely aware of myself. I only knew I was there because I could see my hands and my feet stepping awkwardly in front of me. Like a sleepwalker, I drifted away.

Chapter 27

The following morning, I awoke from a disturbed sleep, still feeling tired. It was an effort to keep back the eager flow of my dark thoughts and I suspected the feeble dam I had built in my mind would soon break. I showered and dressed in my old clothes half-heartedly, tying the laces of my trainers with trembling fingers. The girl in the ice mirror stared back at me with hollow, dark-rimmed eyes.

I wandered out of my cabin as though in a dream; a stranger in my own life. As people passed me, I shrank away, not wishing to speak to anyone or for them to even notice me. This world inside the dome, which I had once found so wondrous, seemed strange and frightening to me, now that I was so alone and lost inside it. My rising confusion seemed to exert a pressure on all my senses until I wanted to scream out loud, and so it was an endless walk until I reached my destination.

As I entered the Centre of Knowing, the many voices of my thoughts began to jabber. Taking a deep breath, I fought to silence them, but not all of them would stay quiet. "This will teach you our history; this place is full of the Knowing," I heard as I remembered Skyen one more time before making my descent into the inky blue world beneath the city. I needed to find out what had gone wrong. There had to be a reason why I arrived back at a different time than before.

What was my destiny to be?

I stepped down the familiar stairs of frozen ice that seemed to materialise out of nowhere. Taking my time lest I fall, I made my way to the bottom, dwarfed in the gigantic cavern and overwhelmed by the glittering lights in the walls. It had slipped my mind how wondrous and peaceful this place was. In the distance I could hear the faint murmur of whale song. It seemed that I now knew how to listen for it.

Stepping on to solid ground, I glanced back up at the circular entrance, just as I had done all that time ago. It was now the teeniest speck. I looked down at my feet, standing as I was on the translucent light blue ice. In contrast to the first time, I was unperturbed.

"There is nothing to fear," echoed Skyen's words in my mind. I remembered him taking my hand and leading me slowly across the frozen floor towards the black water, and I followed once again. Near the edge, I paused and the memory of my guide drifted from my mind.

Within seconds two blue-grey, shiny dolphins bounced up into the air and plunged back down into the sea, splashing me on the way. Their cheerful sounds and free spirit made me smile. I waited patiently as a few more greeted me in the same joyful fashion before disappearing into the abyss. Then he came. I was certain it was the same whale as before. I wondered if he had known I would return here one day. His call filled the silent void and I watched in awe as the powerful, barnacled body of blue surged upwards from the waves. The whale reared up in front of me, seeming to take up the entire space.

Gazing at the mighty creature evoked a memory of that day when I had stood here feeling stunned. I pondered whether he would be so welcoming this time. Droplets rushed off of him, splashing into the dark depths. His song grew louder and then all was quiet as he rested in front of me, motionless. I forced my doubts to the back of my mind and waited for him to speak to me.

"I welcome you to Entyre," I heard him say in my thoughts. "Do not be afraid."

Taking a step forward, I said aloud, "I am not afraid."

"Why have you returned?"

"I came back because," I began, but paused, not knowing how to continue. "I wanted to, needed to."

"You return to a different time."

I sighed. "I know. I wasn't expecting..."

"The people you knew are gone."

"I know... I don't understand."

"The people you knew have returned to the sea; all except one."

"Skyen?" I asked, clutching at the wisp of a hope.

"Have no fear. He is one with the ocean now."

I frowned. "Can I see him?"

"He would not recognise you. He is no longer human."

I stared down at my feet, blinking back tears. My heart plunged. So, it was definitely true. Had I really returned for nothing? Now I was completely alone in this strange world. I chided myself for my weakness; somehow I had to be stronger than this. "What must I do?" I pleaded.

"I do not follow."

I tried again. "What must I do to return to the time that I left?"

"That is a dangerous path that you seek. I warned you once before that time is all we have. You broke the crystal."

"But I did not choose to. Someone else broke it."

"That was unfortunate."

I sighed. "So, what can I do? There must be a way."

There was silence for a while, broken by the flip of a dolphin's tail. I concentrated on keeping my thoughts at bay, imagining that any sudden tumult of fear and confusion in my mind would be sure to deafen the one listening.

"Time bends, but it cannot break," the whale told me after an endless time.

I remained silent, listening.

"You acted with great fortitude in the war..."

"I did?" I gasped. "What war?"

"You fought by the side of your fellow humans."

"B-but it didn't happen," I protested in bewilderment.

"Time bends. It runs in parallel streams as mysterious and as deep as the sea. There is a way, and because of your bravery in battle, I will help you. Such selfless action should always be repaid. There is one way. You must seek The Only."

"The only what?" I asked.

"The Only will guide you. You will find what you seek in the Centre of Knowing. Ask the Keeper for the *Tome of Time*. You will find your answer there."

"Thank you," I replied, humbled but confused. I had not fought in any war.

"I must warn you that you are not the first. The Only may decide not to help you. There will be a bargain to be struck and the power of The Only is mighty. But I wish you well in your journey."

"Thank you. I will try," I said, my voice breaking. "I must."

"Remember that time is all we have. How you live your life is reflected back to you in the waters and this is why I guide you. I bid you leave."

Upon his words the magnificent creature descended into the darkness, disappearing within seconds. Cold water spilled over my feet and I felt completely isolated. I wanted the whale to come back and tell me more, but I knew that he would not. Gazing into the gloomy, rippling surface of the water, I wondered what lay beyond and where Skyen was; what form he now took. I hoped he was at peace. Deep down, I knew that he was.

Chapter 28

Taking a deep breath and harnessing my wits, I turned towards the stairs and ascended the icy blocks to the top. Breaking through the glimmering, I found myself back in the more regular surroundings of the Centre of Knowing. There was something about the place that I found comforting. Glancing around, I noticed the man with short hair, who had helped me the previous day, sorting through some of the ice-thin sheets.

Without thinking twice, I strode up to his desk and greeted him, "Hello."

He looked up, recognition flickering across his face, and asked, "How are you today? Did you find the answers you sought?"

"Think so."

He smiled. "I am happy for that. I was concerned."

"Thanks. Could you tell me where I can find the Keeper?"

The librarian was taken by surprise, but nodded all the same. "Yes. You may find him across the way."

Glancing in the direction in which he was pointing, I noticed a figure in the distance. "Thank you for your help," I said, wandering away.

"Good luck," called the librarian from behind me.

Feeling emboldened, I strode across the floor of the huge building to the other side. As I approached the man, he glanced up and then blinked in surprise. I suspected it was due to my appearance and clothing, which were not of this world. "Good day," he replied. "You are not from Entyre?"

"No, but then I was, and then..." I said, stumbling over my words. "I, err, no, I'm not."

The thin man nodded and his expression softened. He replaced the sheets he was holding on to the bookcase by his side. "How can I help?"

"I spoke with the Balaenoptera, which told me to ask you for the Tome of Time," I announced, deciding to get straight to the point. Even though I felt afraid, I would not show it. I had made a vow to myself to be strong.

For a second the Keeper looked taken aback, but he soon recovered his composure. "That is not a title that is oft requested. Come. Follow me."

The blue-haired man turned and marched further across the room as I trailed behind. I almost had to run to keep in step as he seemed to glide in gigantic strides until he finally stopped in front of a narrow doorway. Passing through the mist, we entered a smaller room lined with rows upon rows of bookshelves, all filled from top to bottom with gleaming strips of sheer ice.

"Come," said the Keeper, and I followed him across the place and down a short flight of frozen steps until we came to yet another doorway. Again it was filled with mist, but this time it was silver.

"This is the place, but I will enter first," he told me. "It will not open for you."

Nodding, I waited for the man to pass through the shimmering before following. The silver was resplendent and I imagined the stars in the sky being made of the same. We entered a room as dark as night, lit by specks of some glittery substance in the walls. I followed the

Keeper to the furthest bookshelf, from which he removed a black box. Upon it was a silver image of a butterfly, looking so real that I almost expected it to flutter off the top before my eyes.

The man took a couple of steps forward and set the box down carefully on a table. Lifting the lid with great care, he glanced at me out of the corner of his eye and announced, "This is the Tome of Time. There are a number of leaves inside. Take the top one. I cannot touch them."

Surprised, but trying to hide it, I peered into the black box as the Keeper stepped aside. With shaky fingers, I reached in and felt the top sheet of ice. It was freezing and appeared to tremble. Gripping the edges tightly with two hands, I removed it and held it up in front of me.

I could feel the interested eyes of the Keeper burning into the side of my face, but the sheet of ice consumed my attention. It was sheer and smooth, but not blue, like everything else. This book was fiery red with streams of yellow that floated across the surface. Trembling slightly, I deciphered the words that seemed to manifest from nowhere. All the time, the man watched me like a hawk, not knowing what I read.

In the place where the earth is as red as blood and the sun drips yellow, you will find The Only. Only she can point the way. The Seeker will find the Path is not an easy one and he will have to face his fears through a series of Tasks, which only he can accomplish in order to go forward. To Return he will have to go full circle. Time is all we have. It bends, but it does not break. To go forward the Seeker must destroy these Words.

"I don't understand," I mumbled, glancing up.

The Keeper raised an eyebrow. "What do you not understand? Is it not clear?"

"It says…"

"No!" he cried, raising his hands. "Do not tell me. The words are for you alone."

"Oh."

Glancing down, I reread the sheet over and over, until the words seemed to ring in my ears. My eyes hovered over the last line. *To go forward the Seeker must destroy these Words.* Frowning, I blinked back my tears as the realization that I was stuck here forever, alone, finally dawned on me. The book made no sense at all. It was just a few lines of nothing. Who was The Only – the only what?

If I was to be trapped in this time, I would rather return home, seeing as I had lost everything here. At least back there I had people who knew me. Tears filled my eyes and I blinked them back, but not until one had run down my face and dripped on to the surface of the glass. It gleamed as the water bounced. For some reason it made me smile. I thought of Skyen's face, which I knew I would never set my eyes on again.

"I cannot leave you alone with the book, but you can sit down and I can turn my back," the Keeper suggested, giving me a look of pity.

I sniffed more loudly than I intended and shrugged. "It doesn't matter. Nothing does."

"But everything matters," the man replied. "You have not deciphered the true meaning of the words. Perhaps they mean something else. Read them again."

"I'm tired of reading," I replied, sitting down beside the desk. Resting the book on my knees, I stared at it once more. The red reminded me of blood and the yellow swimming across it did appear to be as bright as sunlight. It washed over the surface like egg yolk, I thought with a frown. If it were not for the crystal smashing, I would not be in this predicament.

I cursed Yava silently. *How could she?* But she did not know, I reminded myself. She could not know the consequences. The girl was full of hate for me, but she was also acting on her emotions, which were raw. She did not know that I would be cast back to my own time. *Who could imagine such a thing?*

My eyes hovered over the final lines of the text again – '*must destroy these Words*' – and then it struck me. Of course, I had to smash it! I looked at the Keeper, who was still watching me with an almost fatherly expression on his face. I imagined him to be very kind.

"I think I know what I have to do," I told him.

"That is good," he answered with obvious relief. "Do not tell me, however."

"I hope you forgive me if it does not work."

The man's face snapped into a smile. "I shall."

Trembling slightly, I rose to my feet and looked down at the alluring slice of ice. Closing my eyes, I let it slide ever so slowly from my hands. In the darkness I heard a low gasp escape the lips of the Keeper, but he made no effort to move. As if the world was standing still, I stayed silent, not daring to breathe as I awaited the inevitable. A deafening, shattering noise echoed around the walls as the text splintered into what I could only imagine was a thousand pieces, its beauty destroyed forever.

Chapter 29

"What?" I gasped, turning around slowly in a full circle to take in my surroundings. I did not recognise this place. I had expected to return to the city inside the globe, or at least the forest, even the beach, although I had dreaded landing there with the invisible clawed beings. So, where was I instead?

The earth was blood-red, brighter than any soil or sand I had ever seen. Bending down to touch it, I found it to be warm. The sky was a strange shade of orange in which a yellow sun swam. I could hear birdsong, although I saw nothing on the wing. Tall trees stretched upwards, tall and spiky, their limbs filled with bright yellow leaves, shining like gold.

What bizarre place is this?

The grass at my feet was of the brightest green, in sharp contrast to the deep red of the soil. I walked forwards, not knowing where I was or whence I should go. Deep inside, I felt a gnawing sense of dread. My current predicament was my own fault.

I was about to sit down when something landed on my back and began to pull at a strand of my flowing hair. Turning my neck, I gazed down the direction of my spine to see a dragonfly, very long and extremely colourful; a magnificent fire of many shades of crimson. His black eyes turned and he moved up my back to perch on my shoulder.

Though my neck ached from the motion, I continued to gaze down at him, waiting. For such a small creature, he felt uncannily heavy. I moved my arm up slowly, hoping he might choose to run down it, making it easier for me to examine him. The insects here must be unused to people, I thought, as it seemed to have no fear of me.

"Are you lost?"

I checked behind me in astonishment, yet there was not a person there. I looked up and, of course, there was no one in the trees either, and why would there be, but who was speaking?

"I am here."

I almost jumped. *Where is the person hiding?* I swung my head to look down at the dragonfly, which I could still feel on my shoulders. I was amazed that my hair hadn't knocked him off when I looked round. The insect stared at me with his big, inky eyes and blinked.

"I'll ask again, are you lost?"

This time I definitely jumped. It was the dragonfly! He could speak! Or at least it sounded like a 'he'; I couldn't be sure. In a fluster, I sat down heavily on the dry ground and the insect hopped on to my raised knee. Turning, he fluttered his fine wings as a myriad fiery colours danced along his back, incandescent in the sunlight.

"Y-you talk?" I mumbled.

"Why, yes, and you do, too," replied the creature, cocking his head to the side. "But I think you are definitely lost."

I swallowed. Well, I shouldn't be surprised, I told myself. On my last visit away from home, I ended up in a strange forest, being wrestled by invisible hands on a cold beach and rescued by a man who took me down into the depths of the ocean to his world beneath the sea where I communicated by telepathy with a whale. Therefore, a talking insect was really not so unusual, and he seemed friendly enough.

"How can you tell," I asked, "that I'm lost?"

The dragonfly rested his head on one leg. "I know because I have not seen a human in many an age."

"Human?" I asked, my eyes widening. "Aren't there any people here?"

"No."

"Why?"

The dragonfly shook his head. "I do not know the answer."

"Oh."

There fell a spell of silence and I was not sure what to say to break it. Glancing around, the place appeared to be very peaceful. The grass felt soft and damp. Above, the yellow sun continued to blaze brightly, almost dripping like egg yolk. I rolled up the sleeves of my hooded top.

"Where am I?" I asked.

"Jerendali," answered the dragonfly. "First-timer, I presume, so I can give you a tour."

I laughed and the creature looked surprised. "Alright, please do."

"Follow me," he announced with what I imagined was a smile, but it was hard to tell. "You can call me Cidenet."

"My name is Jayne," I added.

The dragonfly flew up into the air and I stood up. It hung there in front of my face. "Ready?" he asked.

I nodded and the polite, colourful thing flew ahead. I walked quickly to keep up as we made our way through the forest. The trees were evenly spaced apart and the soil was still an extremely vivid red, and the green grass very much so. All of the leaves were golden and the bark a deep brown. Continuous birdsong filled my ears and I looked up, hoping to see the singers, but in vain.

"They are hiding because they do not usually see humans," Cidenet explained. "They will come out if they become accustomed to your presence."

"I hope so," I replied, desiring to see them.

I wondered if they would be just as red in colour as this dragonfly. Smiling, I found it funny how everything seemed to match my hair! This new world was so alluring that my fear slipped away easily, as though I was hypnotised by the mellowness of it all.

"This forest is very old and it is called Levandar."

"Are all of the leaves so golden?" I asked.

"Yes. All year round," remarked the dragonfly. "It is never cold here. The sun is always shining."

"That is good to know," I replied, removing my top and tying it around my waist. I wished I was wearing something cooler. Suddenly, I thought of Skyen and my mood plunged. I took a deep breath, willing myself not to think of him now, for I needed to press on and keep my head.

Chapter 30

After about twenty minutes of walking, the trees opened up into a clearing. It was circular, surrounded by a wall of brown bark. In the centre sat a ring of toadstools, which were bright red with yellow dots on top. There were about twelve of them, surrounded by long blades of green grass.

"This is the place of The Only," announced the dragonfly.

"The Only?" I gasped. "That's what I'm looking for."

"I know," he replied, flapping his wings in front of my face.

"How?"

"I can read your thoughts," he replied. Noticing my astonishment and fear, he corrected himself, "Well, not all of them. Just the really strong thoughts."

"I see," I said, trying not to panic and making a mental note not to think of anything too private or embarrassing. "What is The Only?"

"She will approach soon, so we should wait. We can sit on the toadstools here, if you like. She cannot be hurried, you see."

I nodded and followed Cidenet. Walking to the nearest fungi, I felt the rounded cap on top of the stalk, which was strangely soft and kind of rubbery. I took a perch and found it surprisingly comfortable. The dragonfly sat on the nearest toadstool to me, his red hue sparkling in the sun. His delicate gossamer wings glistened.

"Where do you live?" I asked.

The insect looked up, his expression enquiring. "Here and there, and everywhere," he replied. "I have a family, but I do not see them as often as I would like."

"How come?"

"I am always busy," he said. "A flittering here, a fluttering there, a messenger's life is never dull."

"Messenger?"

"Why, yes, I am the messenger of..."

Before he could finish his sentence, a blast of soft yellow petals filled the air and floated downwards, decorating the toadstools and my hair. I closed my eyes as they trickled past my nose. Reopening them, I glanced down at the pieces of flower that now tickled my hands; so soft and silky, they were the same yellow as the leaves on the trees.

"Cidenet, I see you have welcomed our guest!"

I looked up to see the largest, most radiant butterfly that I had ever clapped eyes on. Her wings were a rich golden yellow with tips of brilliant orange, while her body was ebony and her eyes strangely red. As she spoke, her antenna waved in the breeze.

"What is your name," she enquired.

I was certain she smiled and returned my own. "Jayne."

"I am The Only, and I believe you seek me."

I nodded. "Yes, I'm trying to get back somewhere. I left and time seems to have run out..."

The butterfly waved her little legs as she spoke. "Time is very precious. It is the most precious thing we have. You must not take it for granted."

"I didn't mean to," I replied honestly.

"Where is it you wish to return?"

"Entyre. It lies beneath the sea."

The butterfly nodded. "I know of it, the land of water, yes. Their time is different. It flows fast like a current. But you are not of that world."

I breathed deeply. "No, I'm from London, England. Earth…"

The dragonfly flew into the air and hovered, listening intently. "A human named Sophia…"

"You know Sophia?" I cut in, glancing from one creature to the other.

The butterfly nodded. "I met her once. She, too, wished to return to Entyre, but I was unable to grant her wish. She could not change time."

"Can you?" I asked.

The Only fluttered her wings. "No, of this I am unable. No creature can change time, but I can cause a flutter, a void, a break in the threads. Where did you encounter Sophia? It was many moons ago that she passed through here."

"She gave me a magic crystal. It looks as if it has the sea inside and it took me to Entyre."

"But you cannot return because too much time has passed," added the butterfly. "I understand."

"Can you help me?"

"Why do you wish to return so strongly?" asked The Only. "The path you seek is not an easy one. You would be wise to turn back."

"I belong there," I replied, as my breathing grew faint. "I must."

The butterfly's wings flittered. "I see."

Cidenet hovered above the nearest toadstool, watching me intently.

"The path is not simple, but neither is it impossible.

If you fail there is nothing I can do to help you. You must trust in yourself and no one else."

"Anything," I replied with a shrug.

"You are set upon this course?"

"Yes, I am, and I thank you for any help you can give," I answered, trying to sound confident while I trembled inside.

"So it shall be. We will see what the wings of destiny bring you. I shall set you five tasks and you must succeed in each one. Fail once and I will summon you here. Cidenet will be your guide in these dark places."

"What are the tasks?"

"I cannot tell, for they await you only. But I will give you five items of assistance. You must decide which to use and when. The path will take you on a journey, but it will be both a physical and a mental one. Be brave and I wish you success," said the butterfly, holding out a silken bag, tied with a cord of pure gold.

"Thank you," I replied, taking it. To my surprise it was completely weightless. "I can't tell you how grateful I am."

"Be wise and choose carefully," said The Only. "I will see you in five days or fewer. Cidenet, be wary, and do not take any risks. I bid you farewell."

Golden petals filled the air and the butterfly vanished.

"Wow," I breathed. "Thank you for helping me."

The dragonfly bowed his head. "I am the messenger of The Only. I live to serve her. I will be your guide, but you must make your own choices. I cannot aid you here."

Gazing at the golden bag, I nodded in understanding.

Chapter 31

"Where do we go now?" I asked my colourful guide.

"It is your choice alone," replied Cidenet mysteriously.

I nodded. "Okay, so let's go straight ahead."

The dragonfly flicked his wings and flew beside me, neither leading nor following, but hovering just to the side of my right shoulder. I wondered if to offer him a ride, but decided against it. He must be content where he is, I presumed.

Contemplating the intensely green grass dotted in the red earth, I walked at a medium pace; not too fast and not too slow. I did not wish to tire myself, but I also wanted to finish the tasks as soon as possible. It was a mystery to me how many hours had passed since I awoke here. Time appeared to have no place. It was like existing in a vacuum in an unreal world.

As I trod, I stared up at the sky and squinted at the luminous orange. I wondered if I would ever get used to it. The yellow sun shone brightly, its beams spilling into its orange environs. Birdsong filled the trees as we walked. Every now and then I checked the branches, hoping to catch sight of the feathered ones, yet they always seemed to evade me. At times I thought I spotted some movement, but I was never sure if it was just a figment of my imagination.

All around me, the leaves on the trees rustled like whispers and dazzled like gold dust. I wondered if night ever fell, because the sun seemed to glow just as richly as when I'd first arrived. I wandered on, between the spiky branched trees, not knowing where I was headed. Cidenet was silent, but I was soothed by the soft buzzing of his translucent wings. *Was he sleeping as he flew or focused on something I could not see?* Speculating on whether he actually knew what lay ahead, it occurred to me that perhaps this was some kind of trick. I shook my head, which made the dragonfly glance aside at me.

"Don't worry, this is not a trick," he told me, having read my mind. "The Only does not wish you to fail. Her wish is for you to realise your true destiny."

"Okay," I replied, not really knowing what to say or even think.

After a while the pathway forked, leaving me with two optional routes. I stopped and looked to Cidenet for help, but he seemed to shrug and raise an eyebrow. Blinking in surprise, I almost laughed. Eyeing the way to the right, I thought I saw a glowing in the distance. Curious, my feet wandered in that direction.

Perhaps it was just a trick of the light, but there was something moving and it glittered. Gradually it dawned on me that the sunlight was reflecting off something with the appearance of a mirror. I increased my pace and the dragonfly flew a little faster to keep up. He became a streak of flaming red in the corner of my right eye. Always there, his presence soothed me, so I did not worry about the near future.

I walked for what seemed half an hour, as the mysterious object that had seemed so near was actually further away than I thought. As I got closer, so its radiance strengthened. Now I was certain that it was some kind of mirror. Expecting to see my reflection I stopped in front of it, but I saw nothing. Whatever it was resembled a wall of glistening water, covering the path before me, stretching from my feet up into the trees.

The branches overhead curved inwards, forming a type of arch, framing the uncanny shimmering within. I stepped backwards to get my bearings and Cidenet flew that way too. Sure enough, it resembled some kind of entrance, but what sort of doorway was it?

"What do you think, Cidenet?" I asked, observing my companion.

"The real question is what do you think?" he replied, flittering.

I smiled. "I should have guessed you'd say that!"

After investigating my immediate surroundings, I stepped forward and stretched my right hand out towards the mirror-like object. My fingers made contact with a solid veil. Stepping closer, I raised my arm and passed my palm over the cold surface. It seemed to ripple slightly like water, but it was translucent, allowing me to see the forest on the other side.

"I guess we could just walk around it?" I suggested.

"You could," agreed the dragonfly. "Or you could not."

After giving my companion a quizzical look, I studied the glimmering doorway. It resembled a sheet of moving water, as though a breeze blew across it. While it interested me, it raised a sense of dread in me. Removing the little silken bag from my trouser pocket, I examined the contents, looking over at each individual item carefully. The Only had not specified whether I could only use each object once. *Would she trick me?* I turned them over, this way and that. *Which one?*

Looking up, I gazed into the watery thing before me, imagining what it would tell me to do, if it had any senses or a voice, and then I closed my eyes, dipped my hand into the bag and pulled out a grey coloured pebble. It did not sparkle or shine, and was rather dull. Shrugging, I replaced the bag in my pocket and held the stone up to my eyes. I looked sideways at Cidenet, but he was giving nothing away, as usual. He simply buzzed with absolutely no expression on his little face at all.

Turning once more to the mysterious doorway, I extended my arm so the pebble moved closer to the surface. As I did so, the water appeared to ripple around it. Biting my lip, I took the stone even nearer until it touched the water, causing it to bubble, and then to my astonishment my hand sank into the ice-cold substance. I looked at Cidenet and this time he had a big grin on his face, his eyes wide with wonder. He flew closer and perched by my collarbone as I walked towards the eerie, aqueous doorway. It sucked me in.

Chapter 32

A chill ran through me. I was surrounded by water, but I could breathe. My heart beat rapidly as I remembered the two previous occasions when water had consumed me, but I swallowed my fear and kept urging my feet forwards. I closed my eyes, as if to hypnotise myself that everything was fine and nothing would harm me. Oddly, the feel of Cidenet's weight on my shoulder gave me confidence. I pressed forward. After a few, seemingly endless minutes, the chill sensation left me and I felt a tap on my neck.

I opened my eyes to find the dragonfly gazing up at me. "You did well," he told me, smiling, as he circled his wings. He flew off my shoulder and in front of my face, as if he were offering some kind of protection.

"Where are we?" I asked.

I had expected to be on the other side of the watery door, in the green forest with its golden-leaved trees, but instead we were in a dim, chilly cave. The floor was covered in cobwebs, across which tiny spiders crawled, and I cringed. I had never liked the creatures and now I was surrounded by them.

"Cidenet, I'm scared of spiders..."

The dragonfly perched on my shoulder again. "No, you are not. You *were* scared of spiders. Now you are stronger than that."

"If you say so," I muttered, not believing a word of it. My hands clenched in fear.

Stepping forward, I noticed the webs move around my feet, swirling as if they were echoing the natural flow of water, and the walls of the cave appeared to shift also. I wondered if we were indeed underwater, as in Entyre, but I had wandered in from the forest, so I reasoned not. Perhaps it was a gateway to that world I searched for?

Glancing around, I noticed hundreds of tiny creatures covering the walls, perhaps even thousands. It was their motion that made the walls themselves appear to move when in fact they were still. Their little crawling bodies created a rippling along the surface. I edged forward, slowly and carefully, not making a sound. The cobwebs moved away as I approached, and then seemed to close back together behind my feet. Tiny spiders continued to run to and fro, but they avoided touching me. To my relief, they stayed in the webbing.

To the left the cave formed a passageway, which eeled away into darkness. To the right there trailed another. *Which one to take?* I chose the left. My feet moved slowly as I willed them forward into the gloom. I had never been keen on the dark, ever since I was young, imagining the many eerie, supernatural things that could plunge out of it.

The tiny creatures ran across every wall, casting off an almost inky glitter, and I had the impression that they were watching me with their miniscule eyes. Turning the corner, I staggered back in shock as the ceiling quivered and began to move down towards me.

"Back!" I shouted to Cidenet, but he did not obey me. Instead, he flew down to the ground and sat there, looking up at me. "Move! It's going to crush us!" I screamed at him as dust showered me. Wiping it from my eyes, I cursed the insect. I knew I could not leave him. "Cidenet, you'll be the death of me," I said, picking him up.

Not a sound escaped him, but he shook his head at me, silently. Hearing a loud crash, I spun on my heels to see that the way from which I had come was now sealed shut. I ran forward, crouching in instinct as the rock above me lowered itself further. When I was within inches of the place where the passageway turned, it too sealed. I was trapped.

"What's going on?" I shouted, terrified as the space became more cramped. I crouched down on the ground, feeling the claustrophobic pressure.

"You are powerless to stop it," informed the dragonfly, blinking at me.

"Now you tell me," I muttered, lying on the ground.

I flattened my body in a bid to make myself as thin as possible, stretching out my arms and legs amongst the dust. Amid the deafening roar of the rock ceiling grinding against the cavern walls as it came down, I closed my eyes and awaited my fate. Images of my past life swept through my mind, spiralling in a movie reel of my childhood through to the present day as realisation dawned on me that I was not going to leave this place.

Silence. I opened my eyes again in the dead air and spied Cidenet in front of me, his normal blaze of colour muted. My instinct was to sit up, but my head banged against a hard surface: the roof of the cavern, I suspected. Cursing, I tried to move my legs and feet, and discovered they were fine. Ahead there glowed a faint light, which confused me because the passageway had sealed itself earlier.

"Do you know what's going on?" I asked.

The dragonfly shrugged and his delicate wings whirred; he was small enough to fly in the narrow space. Well, you're a lot of help, I thought, as I dug my elbows into the dust and dragged my body forward. As I did so, I felt a weight on my feet and ankles. With a shiver, I tried to turn my head to see what it was, but there was insufficient space. Biting my lip, I hauled myself forward in the direction of the light, yet once more I was distressed to feel something pressing on my legs. It was moving and whatever the thing or things were either multiplied in number or grew bigger, because the weight increased.

My heart began to race. Agitated, I wriggled forward using my elbows. Cidenet flew ahead, pointing to the light in the distance. I nodded, frustrated at the slowness of my progress. Then I heard them. From behind me swept the sound of squeaking, low and constant, accompanied by the flap of heavy wings.

"Bats! Cidenet, there are bats on my legs! I can't move!" I shouted as my breathing came heavier, causing me to cough. I kicked my feet in the narrow space behind me, causing the screeching to intensify.

"Stay calm," my guide advised. "Open your mind."

"Open my mind?" I gasped. "Is that the best advice you can give? I hate bats!"

"I am only the messenger."

"Ugh, if I get out of here...!"

The dragonfly, sensing my rising irritation, flew several feet away from me before turning to watch my progress with interest. I think I cursed him under my breath as I dug in my elbows and tried to drag myself towards him. Feeling the sharp claws of the creatures through the fabric of my trousers, I gritted my teeth as I fought to keep my breathing constant and low. I could not afford to have a panic attack in such a confined area with no one to help me.

It was no use. My limbs suddenly froze. I was stuck. I began to pant loudly, my heart pounding in my throat. Realising that I had to calm myself, I closed my eyes, and tried to concentrate and imagine I was somewhere else, hypnotising my senses. *I can overcome this.* Calming; centring; focusing. *I can fight this.* I embraced the darkness and fixed my attention on ignoring the things that writhed along the lower part of my body, eliminating them from my reality until they no longer existed.

Digging my elbows in, I kept my eyes closed, and focused on my arms as I hauled my body ahead in measured and even movements. Over and over, I dragged and lugged my own weight further forward, not stopping and not allowing my focus to wander. I had one thought in my mind, of reaching the end, and I would let nothing else enter there. On I pressed, enduring the discomfort and pushing my anxiety to the back of everything, so that it ceased to torment me. When I reached the point where I thought I would cry out from the stinging sensation along my rubbed-raw elbows, I felt something brush against my cheek.

Opening my eyes, I saw Cidenet sitting on the ground in front of me. I had reached the light and the passage had opened up once more. Breathing a huge sigh of relief, I dragged myself out from under the heavy rock and stood up. The largeness of the space seemed incongruous at first as I had to get my mind around it. *The bats!* Glancing down at my trousers, I was surprised to find they were not torn. Bending down, I examined my legs and found no scratches. *Did I imagine them?*

"I don't understand," I said, looking at Cidenet. "There were bats scratching me. I felt their claws, but there are no marks."

The insect shrugged. "As you have probably realised, your tasks are to overcome your fears," he replied matter-of-factly, as if it was obvious.

"I see. That's nice," I mumbled, stumbling forwards into the waiting passageway. Whatever; I was just relieved to be out of there. Stretching my legs once more felt good. My head felt in balance again and I swung my arms, glad of the free movement.

When the passageway turned sharply, the light abandoned us. Unexpectedly, I could no longer see anything ahead. I breathed in deeply, puzzled. What on earth was going to happen next?

Chapter 33

Within seconds pitch blackness reined. I would have felt along the walls to guide the way, but I did not want to touch the small beetle-like creatures that roamed there. Instead, I held out both my hands in front of me, palms forwards, and continued to walk. I could just make out Cidenet's dim red colours, but nothing else.

Urging my feet forward, I pressed onwards, making slow progress, until the ground suddenly gave way without warning. I fell. Hearing the soft sound of buzzing, I knew with slight relief that Cidenet was alright and that he was with me. I plunged through the darkness, waving my hands around my head and treading air. My breath caught in my throat and an ice-cold wind sailed past me.

"I am here," said the dragonfly softly as the breeze rippled past my ears.

I was falling and there was nothing I could do. My screams died in my throat. Down, down, down. My hair flew up above my head and something clammy seemed to wrap itself around my waist and creep up towards my neck; a sensation that felt like freezing fingers. I clamped my mouth and eyes shut through fear, telling myself it was probably my imagination. I had to be brave for there was nothing else I could do. This was necessary for me to return. The five tasks had to be completed, I knew this; therefore, I would fear nothing.

The icy hold encircled my neck as I plunged through the darkness, faster and further. *If only there were light; if only I could see where I was going. But would it be any less frightening?*

I swallowed hard as the air blew around my face and under my arms, and the fingers felt their way upwards, around my jaw and cheeks. Another scream was building up inside me, but I dare not let it out, yet it was all too much. I opened my mouth and let my fear come rushing out in a tumult of sound, and as I did so I landed softly, and light flashed on.

Cavern walls surrounded me, but a glittering flickering emanated all around. There were stones in the rock; bright orbs that woke up the dark. I blinked a few times and then turned quickly. Cidenet was fluttering by my side and I breathed a deep sigh of relief, so glad to see my companion was in one piece and with me still.

"I will not leave," he told me softly, as though he had just read my thoughts. I imagined they were easy enough to guess anyway.

The floor of the cave felt cold and hard, but there were no cobwebs. It seemed perfectly clean of anything. Rising to my feet, I brushed myself down and pushed my hair back behind my ears. *Where to go now?* Glancing around, I spotted three passageways, each one leading off in a different direction.

Not knowing why, I had an instinct to take the grey pebble out of the bag again. I did so and held it up in the air. It was no longer dull, but shining, as though it was absorbing the lights in the rock. I turned around slowly and stopped when the stone grew warmer in my hand. Smiling to myself, I replaced it in the bag.

"This way," I said to Cidenet, pointing. Nodding, he flew close to my right shoulder as I headed into the passageway.

Thankfully, the route was lit. Hundreds of little sparkly stones glittered in the slimy-looking walls. The ground looked smooth. I walked steadily, taking each twist and turn calmly, curious as to where the passage would lead and what would befall me next. After walking for quite a way, I stopped at a dead end. Frowning, I felt the wall with my hands, running my palms over the chill surface as though stroking an animal. I could feel the dragonfly watching me. He probably thinks I'm going crazy, I thought.

As I imagined it in my mind's eye, the wall gave way and the passageway continued. Glancing at the insect, I saw him wink and smile. He was impressed, I could tell. Smiling back, I began to walk forward, but as I took those steps I heard the sound of deep breathing rise upwards. I backed against the rock, startled, but the noise became louder until I could feel a soft vibration. *The walls!* I jumped forward and turned. They were subtly moving, as though the cave was breathing. I felt fear glide its way up my spine, turning the hairs on my neck on end.

"Let's go," I said, and the dragonfly buzzed in agreement.

Ignoring the eerie gasping sound and the shifting of the walls, I hurried forward, quickening my pace until I was almost running. My instinct told me that I had to get out of there. The passageway turned and I went with it. After a while it curved again, and then thrice more. I had the eerie sensation that I was walking in a circle. Would I end up where I started? I hoped not.

The cave felt as though it was closing in on me. I would have given almost anything to be outside in the fresh air.

"Come in!"

Chapter 34

I staggered to a stop and spun around, only to find there was no one there. Cidenet, as though sensing my fear, stopped buzzing and perched on my shoulder, his radiant reds glistening in the tiny sparkles of light. I turned around again, more slowly this time, but there was really nothing to see, yet I could have sworn I was being watched. There were eyes on me, deep and probing.

"Come in!" the faceless voice repeated.

"To where?" I enquired, swallowing down my fast rising panic.

The cavern walls began to tremble and I braced myself for another plunge through the dark. I willed myself to be brave as I fought my anxiety. Looking up, I saw sprinkles of dust fall from the ceiling. I dare not look at the ground, imagining a huge pit was about to open up. Instead, I felt a tugging at my feet. Glancing down, I saw a pair of hands, their fingers long and bony, the skin the colour of dead fish, and inky black fingernails.

"Ah!" I screamed and tried to move backwards, but I was frozen to the spot, gripped as if by hooks.

"Don't fear it," whispered Cidenet. "Open your mind."

"I am opening it," I replied, almost wanting to flick him off my shoulder. I wished he would speak straight for once, although I realised he couldn't. He was only the messenger after all.

Glancing up at the ceiling and the walls, my heart sank as there was nothing to hold on to. I would not be able to raise myself up. Cursing under my breath, I looked down at the wrinkled hands. The skin seemed to have an oil-like texture, as if the top layer was gliding over the one beneath, and I shivered. The black nails seemed as sharp as razors. I tried once more to wriggle, but I was not going anywhere. Closing my eyes, I waited for the inevitable.

"Come in!" the voice said again, and then an icy, cutting chill ran through my body, from my feet all the way up to the top of my head. It was so bitter that it seemed to burn, but it only lasted a second for at the very moment that I opened my mouth to scream the sensation stopped.

I cracked open my eyes. Cidenet was sitting silently on my right shoulder and we were in a cavern. There was light here, from the sparkles in the dank walls again, but they were blue this time; the steady glow of aquamarine stones. There she was, staring at me with an expression unfathomable; her long fingernails hanging from grey, loathsome hands draped over the seat in which she sat. I so wanted to peel my eyes away from her, but I knew I should not. I had to face this.

"You came," she remarked in a tone that seemed to sear the cavern air in two.

I stared at her hair, which appeared to be made of seaweed. It hung in clumps all the way down to her knees, wrapping itself around her body in waves of black, as though it were alive. I imagined hundreds of creatures living inside, feeding on it.

"How did you know how to get in?" she asked.

Her eyes seemed to burn through me into my very

core. Dark orbs, lifeless and dull. Her skin was translucent, like grey, dank water, and I could see the bones beneath. It was as if a skull were talking to me, but a living, breathing one.

"I walked in," I answered, willing my legs not to shake. I could not run away, even if I tried. Fear had me rooted to the spot.

"I see," she remarked and then cackled, grey slithers of drool spilling from her lips.

I shivered, but stood my ground, feeling that she was my only way out. The dress that she wore resembled cobwebs; layer upon layer of webbing on which those familiar, tiny black spiders raced up and down, and to and fro. Upon her feet were... I expected black slippers, but she had no feet. There was nothing below those webs. Her legs appeared to just end.

Noticing where I was staring, she snapped two of her grey, lifeless fingers together. The sound bounced off the walls and echoed around the chamber. I wondered what Cidenet was thinking at that moment, and if he was feeling the same emotions as me. Not daring to speak, I peered all around out of the corners of my eyes while keeping my focus on...

I could not call her a woman. She showed no resemblance to any female I had ever seen before. I wondered if she was a witch or dead even, suspended somehow between this life and another, or if she were some creature from the sea. Her skin rippled like dank water as she raised her bony arms together, the thin hide barely concealing the skeleton beneath.

She lifted from the chair and glided towards me, the cobwebs spilling out all around her. The blue light made her skin seem greyer and the black strands of her hair drifted, as though she were swimming in the sea. As she approached, I found that I could not move my stare from her eyes, even though I tried. My hands became rigid fists by my sides as her face drifted to within inches of my own. I swallowed, my breath trapped in my throat. I felt as if my heart would stop, here and now, in this dark cave with this loathsome thing floating in front of me.

"Bring me the heart of the unicorn," she said, grey bile dripping from her lips as her pungent breath wafted over me. It smelt of the dead. Still, dank and suffering. I suddenly imagined her in a crypt, the stone coffin sealed forever and her enclosed inside, washed out into the sea. Nothing lived, nothing thought, everything defunct.

I blinked once and she was gone, along with everything else; the passage, the blue lights, the cave. Everything had disappeared. I was standing in the forest where tall trees stretched up towards an orange sky and their yellow leaves twinkled in the yellow sun. The grass was green and the earth was red. I exhaled. It was a deep sigh of relief, as if I had not breathed in days. Drawing the fresh air into my lungs, I sank to my knees.

Chapter 35

"Are you alright?"

Brushing my red hair out of my eyes, I saw Cidenet fluttering in the air with an unreadable expression. I nodded, unable to speak for a moment. The eyes of the crone were seared into my mind. She was still there in my thoughts, haunting me. I shook my head as if to shake her out, and lay back on the grass to gather my composure. Smiling, I gazed up at the flickering dance of the light on the leaves, proud of myself for facing the hag and standing my ground. Surely that was something?

"Look behind you," said the dragonfly.

Rolling over on my front, I leaned on my elbows and recognised the glimmering doorway behind me, framed by the brown branches of the bowing trees. The archway still stood and the watery surface continued to ripple in its eerie mystery. For some reason I laughed.

"What has amused you?" asked my companion.

"I don't know, Cidenet. Honestly, I have no idea. I'm just so happy to be out of there. Was she dead?"

The dragonfly shook his head. "She was alive, or as alive as she could be."

Frowning, I bit my lip. "Either she is or she isn't…"

"Sometimes something can be two things at once. Not everything is one thing."

"Cidenet, what are you talking about?" I asked, shaking my head. "Please talk simply."

"Why?" he asked, buzzing lightly on the wind. "It is more interesting this way, no?"

"Definitely no," I replied, giggling. Standing up and brushing my clothes down, I looked straight into his eyes. "I think you confuse me on purpose."

"I am only the messenger," he stated, "and things are not always what they seem in this world and the others." Cocking his head to one side, he sped up his wings so they whirred.

"Cidenet, you are very funny," I told him, walking ahead. My companion buzzed behind me and then caught up to my side, hovering by my shoulder as always.

I stopped. "I just remembered what she said. She asked me to bring her the heart of the unicorn."

The dragonfly's red skin shimmered. "Yes, she did say that."

"But she doesn't expect me to kill a unicorn, does she? How could I? There's no way," I announced and then paused to think. "Do unicorns even exist? Where I come from they are the stuff of fairy tales..."

"Indeed, they exist," Cidenet interrupted. "They are as real as you or I."

"But you're a talking dragonfly. I sometimes think you might not be real and that I'm dreaming."

To my astonishment, my companion chuckled. His red body became even brighter and his wings whirred faster.

"You're laughing! You're actually laughing?"

The dragonfly replied by chuckling some more.

"Okay," I gave in, "so the joke's on me, but, seriously, how can I kill a unicorn? I've never even seen one. I couldn't kill an animal. It isn't in me."

"They are rare," Cidenet remarked. "I believe there is only one left in this world."

"One?!" I gasped. "Then I certainly can't kill it. That old woman or thing, or whatever she is, is just evil."

"But she has set you one of the five tasks," my companion reminded me. "If you want to succeed then you must complete all of them."

"But, I can't kill it. That's ridiculous. How can..?"

"I am only the messenger. I cannot guide you," he replied.

"Yes, yes, I know," I muttered, rolling my eyes.

For the next half hour or so, I was oblivious to my feet moving, one in front of the other, so deep in thought was I. There was one question on my mind: was I capable of killing? In the past I had inadvertently trodden on the odd snail or beetle, and even swatted a fly or squished a spider out of fear, but could I kill a creature?

Were they the same thing? Was an insect just as important as an animal? Was it just as sophisticated in thought and everything else? Cidenet was a dragonfly, after all, so he was an insect and a very intelligent one. I decided then and there that I would have more respect for the smallest of creatures in future, wherever I ended up.

"I see you are worrying," he said out of the blue, as though catching his name in my thoughts.

"Yes," I said, looking up. "I cannot kill a..."

"So do not pay it any more thought," advised the dragonfly. "What will come will come – if it is your destiny, so it shall be."

I gave my companion a half-smile. His words were wise, but unfathomable. Everything that passed his lips could have at least two different meanings, but I decided to take the essence of what he said and not pay the dilemma any more thought.

As we continued our walk, the forest disappeared. The bright scenery around us did not alter subtly; it just vanished, replaced by a wide lake. I looked at Cidenet for an explanation, but he gave no reaction at all. I guessed that some magical force was to blame for the change, which might even be an illusion, unable as I was to think of any other plausible reason.

The water in the lake was dark and dank with a pungent smell that reminded me of rotting vegetables. Glancing around, I noticed how different the trees were in this place. Their faded leaves were almost colourless and their limbs still stretched upward, but their appearance was more jagged. They made me think of spectres.

Above my head, the yellow sun was no more and the once orange sky now resembled blood. The lively birdsong had fallen silent. I had the feeling that everything stopped in this place, which should not really be here. Death seemed to walk, haunting the greyness and the ever-darkening deep of the water. Stepping towards the edge, I stared down, but I received no reflection.

"This is for you."

I turned quickly to see a giant stag beetle. His long antennae flicked and he held something between his claws. Crouching down, I peered closer at the little fellow. Well, less of the little as he was pretty big for a beetle. His shiny abdomen and thorax were covered in yellow and brown spots, while his head was jet black. I noticed that his eyes though tiny were very bright. As he stretched out his front claws towards me while supporting himself on his hind ones, I carefully took the piece of paper.

"May The Only be watching you," the creature said before scurrying away.

"It must be a message," I said, standing up.

Flying closer, the dragonfly peered over my shoulder as I opened the yellowish paper. It had been folded over and over, and turned out to be of a much larger size than expected. The writing was clear and curvy, and in a golden hue, which shone amongst the grey surroundings.

"This is your task. You must release the mermaid from the depths of the lake. Fail in this and your true destiny can never be," I read aloud.

A shiver ran up my neck as the meaning of the words sank in. I would have to dive into the lake. I dropped the paper and turned to Cidenet. "I can't," I muttered, tears filling my eyes. "I can't."

The dragonfly flew in front of me and looked into my eyes. "Don't cry. I think you can do anything that you set your mind to."

I slumped to the ground and rested my elbows on my knees. "You don't understand. I nearly drowned. I was in hospital and I couldn't... I couldn't walk again. I died, Cidenet, for some minutes."

"That was in the past."

"Yes, but I can still remember the water and not being able to breathe..." I paused and shivered as tears trickled down my cheeks. I brushed them away with the backs of my hands.

"I know your sadness," said the dragonfly. "I can feel what you feel."

"You can?" I asked, looking at him.

"It is my gift. As well as hearing your thoughts, I can feel your emotions," he added. "If I choose to, but usually I give you privacy."

"Well, thanks," I replied, sniffing. "I don't want you to think I'm weak."

Cidenet shook his head. "I do not think you are so, but quite the opposite in fact. You entered the cave and you spoke to the..."

"What? Who did I speak to?" I asked. My tears had stopped and now I was curious. What was he holding back from me?

"I cannot say..."

"I know. You are only the messenger," I replied. "Okay, so my fate depends on this," I continued, almost to myself and not expecting an answer.

Standing, I brushed down my clothes and wandered back to the water's edge. It was eerie how the surface did not reflect anything, even my face. It was unfathomable. I wondered how deep it actually was and imagined the black silence below. Fear was a frightening thing in itself, I knew; probably the most intimidating emotion in the world, stifling an action before it could begin; preventing thought, feeling, ambition...

I shrugged. The key was not to think. Closing my eyelids, I turned my imagination to pleasant things. I thought of him. He was waiting, somewhere, there in the past, present or future. I was not sure which, but he was there. I sensed he was not lost to me forever. He could not be. *What would existence hold for me if he was gone?*

In the dark shadows, I admonished myself for thinking that everything depended upon one person. It dawned on me that even if I could not return to him, life would go on. Even if he was lost to me, there were other reasons to live. He was my first love and I felt it deeply, and I knew it would endure, but I was still a person apart from him.

I promised myself that no matter what, I would live for myself and every new day. This adventure would be mine. Life was a gift and it was there to be enjoyed or endured, no matter what circumstances threw up at me. I would never forsake such a great gift, especially as destiny had opened the door for me to experience more than one life journey. I recalled Sophia's words: time is all we have.

I opened my eyes and turned to the dragonfly, who was perched on a stone, watching me. "I am ready," I said softly. "I have to do it now or I never will."

Chapter 36

The insect did not reply, but only nodded, as though he realised that speaking would break the spell that now surrounded me; this confidence woven by my determination and my blind faith in my own fortune. Everything happens for a reason, I told myself. Somehow, whatever occurred, I would not change. Even if I failed these tasks, I would have tried, and as one door closed, I knew another would open, as my grandfather always said. And I would still be me.

Quickly, I removed my clothes until I was just wearing my underwear. Without pausing to look at my companion, I strode defiantly towards the water's edge, took a deep breath and plunged through the dark surface. Coldness crept into my bones as I swam down into the eerie depths. I ignored it and focused on making even strokes with my arms. Down through the pitch I dived, reeds catching at my legs and arms, swishing in circular motions.

Down below, it was not so dark, but silence reigned, along with the biting cold. Holding my breath, I glanced around. It was too long a time. Kicking my legs, I soared up to the surface where I gasped for air, before diving down again. Do not think, I told myself. I just swam.

The dark green reeds were thick and clutched at my limbs as I searched the area of the lake closest to shore. A shoal of silver-scaled fish swept past my face and I was surprised at this sign of life in such an austere place. Turning, I pushed on in the other direction, checking along the edge of the lake and then rising to satisfy my lungs.

Treading water, I spied Cidenet waiting in the same place as before. He had not moved an inch. Smiling, I swam out towards the centre of the lake. As I trod water, the immensity of it filled my thoughts, battering at my senses and filling them with anxiety. I swallowed it down, pushing my rising fear to the very back. Clearing my mind, I tried to think of nothing. It seemed to work. Then I imagined that I was not here, not really. I was someone else and only watching the swimmer. It was not me and I was not cold; I was not afraid.

Taking a deep breath, I made another plunge, down as far as I could manage. The underworld seemed a little lighter, but I could not find what I was looking for. Kicking upwards for air yet again, I made my way towards the farthest shore and trod water for a few seconds to regain my strength and fill my lungs.

Diving again, I noticed something in the shadows of the reeds. It was twisted and looked like a box of some kind. As I swam closer, I realised that it was made of stone. Like a casing, it had a lid. I pushed the top with all my might and to my astonishment it slid off easily. Inside was a woman.

Her eyes opened slowly and stared back at me. Her hair was long and flowing, like grass seeping in the water, and her pale face was delicate and impish. As I continued to stare, the woman's lips turned up into a smile, which made me shudder. I became grimly aware of the time I had spent underwater in this deathly place.

Swimming backwards, I beckoned the stranger to

follow. Desperate for air, I swam upwards as fast as I could handle, not even looking to see if she was behind me. As I broke the surface, I gasped and took in several deep breaths. The sky seemed to be a darker shade of blood red than before. I spied Cidenet, still sitting patiently on a stone.

As I trod water, the lady with the flowing hair appeared beside me, smiling from ear to ear, her eyelashes blinking away the dank water. Her hair was the colour of fresh limes and her eyes were yellowish. I was not sure if it was the light, but her skin appeared to be a light shade of green as well. She laughed suddenly and said something that I did not understand, and then swam towards the shore.

I followed quickly, kicking back my legs, but unable to match her speed. The sensation of swimming was no longer so frightening to me. I realised that I had faced my deepest fear and broken it.

"You saved me," the lady said as I reached the shoreline.

"You're welcome," I replied, unable to think of anything else. "How long have you been trapped there?"

"I do not know," she answered, gazing down into the water. "A long time. Forever, it seemed."

I climbed up on to the grassy shore and dried myself with my hooded top. I needed to get warm. There was still the task of the unicorn's heart, but I had all the time in the world it seemed to me. I dressed quickly in my jeans, vest, socks and trainers. The top was too drenched to wear, so I tied it around my waist.

Turning, I went to help the lady out of the lake, but she waved me away. Oddly, she used her elbows, which she dug into the soil, to haul herself upward. Where she should have had legs was a long, glistening green tail. I stared in amazement as it swished, sending splatters of water into the dank lake.

"You're a mermaid?" I asked, sure that my eyeballs were popping out of my head.

"Yes," the lady replied with a mystical smile. "My name is Ethynaryn," she added, moving her tail onto the land and brushing back her lime-green hair with her hands. I was struck by her eyes, which appeared to shine like gold, so unreal were they.

"Do you know how you got there?" I asked.

The lady just nodded and glanced backwards into the watery distance. I wondered what her secret could be.

"Do you know where the unicorn is?" I blurted out.

"I have been in the water too long," she replied. "I do not recall."

"Sorry," I answered, feeling foolish.

Glancing at Cidenet for help, I was met by a bemused expression on his face. I half-expected him to laugh. I could see that he was waiting for me to decide what to do next.

"Where did you live?" I asked after a while. "I can help you to get there."

"There is one place you could take me," Ethynaryn replied, searching my eyes.

"Where?"

"Into the forest by the watery gate," she said softly.

I gazed down at the green scales that seemed to move along her tail. "But how can you get there...?"

"You will have to carry me. Do you think you can?"

I doubted it very much, but the hope in her eyes made me want to try. "I'll try," I offered, bending down.

Ethynaryn placed her clammy arms around my

neck, and I slid my own under her tail and around her waist, and lifted. I was amazed to find that she weighed nothing at all. Laughing, I scooped the mermaid up in my arms and nodded to Cidenet. "Coming?"

"Of course," he replied. "I am curious as to your next move."

"Of course you are," I said, giggling. "Ethynaryn, tell me about yourself..."

"There is not much to tell," she replied, as I walked across the dark grass.

The sky above seemed even bloodier as I trod carefully, willing myself not to trip. I had not taken many steps when the scenery flickered, giving way to the brightly coloured forest of before. The radiance of the sun made me squint. Once more we were back in the comforting world of an orange sky, red earth and yellow leaves. I welcomed it.

"I am the daughter of a king," Ethynaryn said after a while. "I remember now. Everything is cloudy in my mind, but I do know this. My mother died when I was born." A tear slid down her cheek. "It is as if it just happened. How strange..."

"Memories are like that," I remarked. "Sometimes I think of things that occurred a long time ago, and it feels like only yesterday, and I feel it so."

"The mind is a strange creature," Cidenet agreed.

The mermaid smiled at the dragonfly. "I have an idea that you are wise," she said. "Who are you?"

"I am just the messenger," he replied, and the girl looked puzzled.

"Here we are," I said at last as I spotted the watery doorway between the bowing trees. "Where now?"

"Can you walk through?" asked Ethynaryn.

"I don't know. I had to use a stone before and it led to an awful place."

The mermaid looked at me. "I just know that I am meant to go through it. There is a witch in the cave."

"You know?" I gasped. "So she is a witch!" I glanced at the dragonfly, who looked away.

"Have you met her?" the mermaid asked.

"Yes, it is because of her that I asked you about the unicorn. She frightened me."

"Really? I know that she is a powerful witch. Did she seem so to you?"

"Yes, but is this one of your past memories? Have you been here before?"

"I do not recall, but I do know she is one of the most powerful beings in the forest. My father told me and maybe she can guide me home," the mermaid recalled. "But I forget..."

"Let's try then," I agreed after a while, "if you are sure. She terrified me though."

The dragonfly flitted on to my shoulder and I spied his blazing red out of the corner of my eye. Taking a deep breath, I stepped forward into the watery doorway and it swallowed me up once more.

Chapter 37

Opening my eyes, I recognised the inside of the cave whose floor was covered with cobwebs, upon which raced tiny black spiders. "Here I am again," I muttered, half to myself.

"Can you put me down?" asked the mermaid.

"On the ground with the spiders?" I asked, remembering my arachnophobia.

"Of course," she replied.

Shrugging, I lowered the girl to the floor. As I did so, the spiders ran away and the cobwebs parted. Beneath, the ground was clean.

"Thank you," said Ethynaryn. "You can leave me now. I owe you my life. You have my eternal gratitude. Perhaps I can help you find your unicorn afterwards."

"No," I replied, unable to abandon her to the loathsome crone. "I'll stay with you to make sure you are safe."

"So be it. I will call her."

The mermaid began to sing a soft song of longing. I listened as the words undulated around the cavern, echoing off the walls. The hairs on the back of my neck stood on end and I was not sure if it was caused by the thought of the witch appearing or the song itself. My question was answered when the hag flew into the room, the cobwebs drifting out around her and her black hair streaming like oily tendrils that were alive. I recoiled, tearing my eyes away from the skull with the dead eyes in terror.

The mermaid turned to face the witch and opened her arms towards her. "Odirine..."

"I thought you were dead," the hag replied with a scowl across her skull-like temple. "You were meant to be."

Meant to be? Did she know? I forced my feet not to move.

"I put you in the stone chest myself," the crone said in a voice that made the walls tremor.

So she did intend to kill the girl, but why?

"I am a mermaid. I could breathe in my prison beneath the water," explained Ethynaryn. "I did not die."

"How many years has it been?" the hag appeared to ask herself.

"Too many," the mermaid stated. "I do not recall. The days, months, years all blended into one longest time, and it was so dark inside."

"But it was the route of least suffering," the hag replied, her black hair twisting around her body as she hovered in the hair.

Looking to where the witch's feet should have been, I saw nothing there. I wondered how she flew. She cast a deadly look at me and I glanced away.

The mermaid's tail flopped. "Do you have water?"

The witch raised her arm and a column of refreshment fell from the ceiling, soaking Ethynaryn from head to toe. "Thank you," she said. "You are kind."

"Kindness is only for the weak," the crone scoffed, before rising higher into the air. She opened her mouth wide and an arctic wind chased around the cave. I wrapped my now dry hooded top around my shoulders and hugged myself.

"You betrayed me!"

"I did not. I was only true to myself," protested the mermaid. "You know this."

"Insolence! You know nothing. You betrayed me and your mistake will be rewarded in kind." With that the witch rose higher into the air, the cobwebs spiralling down on which the spiders played. She clicked her black fingernails together and a blade of ice flew down into the floor.

"But I did not betray you!" the mermaid cried out as she moved away.

The hag retaliated by sending another channel of ice crashing into the floor of the cave on the other side of the girl.

"Do you think we should leave?" whispered the dragonfly into my ear.

I gazed around the cavern. "No," I replied. "She is helpless."

"Do you not remember?" asked the mermaid loudly.

"I remember everything," screamed the witch. Clapping her hands together, a sturdy sword resembling a sharp-ended icicle appeared in her grip. "So now you must pay with your life."

Ethynaryn did nothing, but sigh, "If it must be."

"No!" I cried, running forward as the cruel hag lunged at the girl on the ground. Reaching out her bony fingers, she grabbed my wrist and spun me around in the air, my legs flying out. Struggling to free myself, I found that she was too strong. The grey, translucent skin on the hand grasping my arm seemed to glide in bubbles. Dizziness yawned over me and I dropped to the ground like a stone. The dragonfly buzzed towards me, but the hag waved her hand, sending him flying into the rock.

"Cidenet! No!" I cried, scrambling across the floor of the cave.

The insect looked up at me and I could not read his expression. He lay still, but I had the feeling that he was pretending. I crawled around to see the bony face of my enemy gazing at me with a look of pure hatred. She had clearly lost interest in the mermaid for now. Ethynaryn, to my astonishment, had not moved. The girl lay there, weakly awaiting her dark fate. *Why did she not do something?* I realised that I would have to fight for both of us.

A bony hand shot up and a slice of glistening ice shot past me. I dodged it, almost losing my balance in the process. The hag laughed. "Dance, little girl!"

Another icy blast came my way and I backed against the cavern wall, so rough and slimy to my touch. Catching my breath, I sought a potential weapon. My eyes spotted a pile of rocks in the corner and I raced towards them as a sharp slither embedded itself in the ground behind me. Out of the corner of my eye I caught a flash of red; Cidenet must have recovered himself. Grasping one of the biggest rocks I could manage, I rushed back, keeping to the edge of the cavern, all the time gazing up at the hag, who continued to circle in the air.

"What have you there?" she asked, cackling at me.

"Nothing," I replied, creeping away towards the mermaid, whom I felt bound to protect.

"You need not help me," Ethynaryn said softly.

Ignoring her words, I moved in front to guard her. The witch laughed and pointed a bony finger at me. She swooped down swiftly and floated a few inches from my eyes, confident of my weakness in comparison to her strength. No fear wrote itself upon her face, no care. I imagined she felt nothing inside. As she drew closer, I raised the rock, but she seized my wrist and shook it, before sending me flying to the side. I landed heavily and an ache pounded through my back. I glanced at Cidenet. For the first time he looked concerned.

The mermaid crawled slowly towards me, her tail, so useless here, flapping in the air. "This is my fate. You cannot stop it," she told me. "It is as it is. Do not risk yourself."

"But I saved you. I can't leave you," I pleaded.

"And I am grateful, but this is my fate. You must go. The water..."

Water? Of course! I reached into my pocket for the golden-coloured bag and twisted it open with shaking fingers. Almost dropping it in my eagerness, I fished out the dull stone. *If it is water then surely..?*

I held the pebble up in the air and made to throw it. In a flash, the witch twisted around to look at me, a wretched look of terror on her face. So the stone contained magic of some kind, I realised, and she feared it. If it opened the entrance, I surmised that perhaps it would help me find a way out, but would it kill her? There was only one way to find out.

"Where did you get that?" wailed the horror that turned this way and that in the air.

I stared at her in silence, my hand raised. Taking a step back, I put all my power into throwing it.

"No!"

Staggering forward, I turned to see Cidenet flying straight at me. He had stopped me, but he was not meant to. It was written all over his face. He was not meant to decide for me; he was only the messenger. Dropping my arm, I stared at him in anguish as he fluttered to my side. "Why?"

The dragonfly looked towards the witch and my eyes followed. Her expression gnarled, she flew backwards into the cavern wall, which trembled. Dust travelled down to the floor. The crone covered her face with her grey, bony hands; the dark fingernails digging into the thin skin covering her skull as she wailed. Around her head the dark tendrils wriggled freely, moving with a life of their own, twisting downwards like snakes until they surrounded her entire body. Whether they were protecting or attacking, I could not tell.

The witch rose up higher, towards the ceiling, until she was cast in the corner like a dark spider. Whether creeping into a defensive pose or getting set to attack us, I had no idea, but I feared the worst.

Placing the stone back into the golden bag, I gripped it tightly, fearful of dropping it. My legs shook from adrenalin and my throat was so dry that it blanched. The mermaid was looking up at the witch with an expression resembling pity, but why? I did not understand. I wished Cidenet would speak, but, predictably, he was silent.

As I turned to walk towards Ethynaryn, the crone suddenly swept down towards us with an eerie, bloodcurdling scream, her arms outstretched and her bony face wracked with hatred. In horror, I froze. "I remember," she cried out and the cavern itself began to quake.

A series of echoes bounced off the walls and all of the spiders scurried into the darkest corners. The cobwebs followed, sliding across the surface of the ground like a wave. The hag drifted down and glided about an inch from the ground.

"You see, I did not betray you," said Ethynaryn, her eyes brightening.

"You did not defend yourself..."

"I cannot..."

"I almost killed you," the witch groaned, her face torn with self-loathing.

"I know... again, I..."

The hag spun her head to meet my face. "And you almost killed me!"

I glanced down at the bag in my hands. *The stone?* I peeked at Cidenet out of the corner of my eye. You stopped me, I thought, knowing he would hear if he was listening, and I knew...

"I remember," said the witch, stretching out her bony arms towards Ethynaryn. "I am you!"

As she spoke the words, the cavern instantly filled with water, surging strong and fast. I coughed and spluttered as the liquid slipped into my mouth and up my nostrils. My hair flowed outwards and my eyes stung, and then just as suddenly, the whirlpool was gone again. The air filled with the sound of the sea, as though I were listening to its rush through a shell that I had found on the beach, soft and flowing. I closed my eyes as my head seemed to spin. Dizziness overtook me and I collapsed.

Chapter 38

"Wake up... wake up..."

The soft voice echoed in my dreams a few times, hanging in the air above me, and then I awoke. Blinking, I rubbed my eyes and recalled where I was: the cavern. "Cidenet?"

"I am here," he said, his voice soothing in its familiarity. I smiled as I spotted the insect on the ground by my side. Of course, he had not left me for a moment.

"How are you feeling?" asked the voice again.

My eyes steadily focused on another face, which was soft, round and impish. Her skin was very pale like snow and her hair long and golden. The full, pink mouth curved into a smile, accompanied by dimples, but it was her eyes that drew me. They were golden with streaks of a deeper bronze within.

"It's you," I gasped, sitting up.

"Don't fret, it is indeed me, Ethynaryn," she said, stroking the hair back from my face. "How are you feeling?"

"Dazed. What happened?" I asked, noticing the cave was empty. "Where is she?"

"The witch?" asked the girl, raising an eyebrow. "She is no longer here. Well, her appearance is gone, but she is inside me now."

"I don't understand."

"We were the same person, but divided by a spell; the charm of a cruel mind. Yet it was a two-handed incantation – while cruel, it was also designed to protect," she added with a half-smile.

"I still don't..."

"You will," she replied, soothingly. "The spell broke us in two. I was imprisoned in the lake and the witch was trapped here. Neither of us retained any memory of the other for so many, many years. She became twisted and, I think, I became numb. I only remembered her after you rescued me, but I could not tell her who I was. I had to wait for her to recognise me."

I sat in silence, turning over my thoughts. *A person divided in two.*

"You stopped me from throwing the stone," I told the dragonfly with a frown. "But you are only the messenger, not..."

"I have no understanding of what you speak," replied Cidenet tartly. "I did nothing of the kind. You decided for yourself."

I squinted at him, but decided not to say another word. I hoped The Only was not listening or saw her servant assist me. "I remember now," I replied cautiously, "it was me who decided not to throw it. I think my head was fuzzy."

"You should not give others credit for your own wisdom," added the dragonfly.

"Ah, well, that reminds me," said Ethynaryn, getting up and walking away, her long, white robe trailing along the ground behind her.

"You have legs!" I gasped.

"Yes," she said, turning, "thanks to you. Have you not noticed how different this place is? We are no longer in a cave. This is my father's house."

As I scanned the cavern, it began to change before

my eyes: the darkness was replaced by light, the dusty floors with polished marble, and the walls seemed to paint themselves in vivid colour as my gaze swept the room. From the ceiling intricate silver chandeliers were suspended, filled with lit candles. Reds, greens and purples now decked this chamber, which was huge and glorious, decorated with many beautiful paintings. Noticing a sumptuous chaise longue right by us, I jumped up and sat on it.

After watching Ethynaryn leave the room by an old, oak door, I turned my head and discovered we were no longer alone. Some people were seated at the far end of the room, playing a game on a wooden table, while a dog barked in the corner with a young boy, who giggled.

"Are we really in the same place?" I asked, blinking.

The dragonfly nodded. "We are. I have to say this seat is rather comfortable. You did well. You saved the Lady of Nyla. Her father had long mourned his daughter. Now time has returned to the day before she vanished and he will mourn no more."

I smiled, knowing as I did that I would have failed in my task if it were not for my small friend. The sound of footsteps made me turn to the door. It was Ethynaryn, carrying a purple box. She perched herself on the chaise longue beside us.

"You must allow me to give you a gift of thanks," she told me with a huge grin. "And I will not take no for an answer."

"I am happy to accept," I replied, smiling back.

The small box felt like velvet. Edged with gold, it was surprisingly heavy, and I rested it carefully on my lap. A small, golden key poked out of an ornate lock at the front. Curious, I went to turn it.

"Do not open it," instructed the girl.

"What's in it?" I asked. "I love presents."

"It is what you seek – the heart of the unicorn."

"Oh!" I gasped as my hands instinctively recoiled.

"Do not worry," Ethynaryn said, noticing my anguish. "We did not harm the unicorn. The witch was guarding the heart, protecting it from the wrong hands, but yours are the right ones and I confidently give it to you."

"What should I do with it?" I asked.

"You must take it to the unicorn..."

"The unicorn, but isn't this the..."

"There is one left. You must find it and give the box to him. He has lost his heart and he has been searching for it everywhere. Only you can take it to him. You must protect it with your life," she replied ominously.

I stared down at the box: another task. "I will," I answered, looking up. "Do you know where he might be?"

The Lady of Nyla sighed as she shook her head. "No. According to legend, the last time he was seen was on the edge of the forest where the clouds meet the sea. You might start there."

I glanced at Cidenet. "Do you know the way?"

"Where the clouds meet the sea?" asked the dragonfly. "Indeed I do."

Chapter 39

The sun's brightness had begun to fade by the time we reached the edge of the forest, which answered my question as to whether it ever set in this place. Yet the day had seemed to be much longer than the ones I was used to at home. I carried the box in my right hand and Cidenet hovered by that shoulder all the way, as though he were guarding its contents from harm. The black bag with my precious gifts from The Only was safely in my trouser pocket.

Where the tall, lush trees ended, we now stood upon the edge of the sea, which lay still and tranquil. In this idyll, waves lapped softly against the thin beach, rippling back and forth. Tiny droplets of surf were carried inward and then abandoned on the orangey sand.

"Wow, it's beautiful," I remarked, gazing at the birds, which circled and whooped playfully in the dying light. "But I thought the sky met the sea here."

Cidenet smiled. "It does, but it is not time."

"So when will that be?"

"Have patience. We can sit on the beach and look out at the sea," suggested the dragonfly. "It will not be too long a wait."

I should have guessed that a straight answer was out of the question, but then I wondered if my companion was actually unsure of the right time. Perhaps he had no idea and was just guessing. I smiled to myself as I wandered on to the sand. Removing my trainers and socks, I sat down and pushed my toes into the cool, dampness around me, feeling at peace for the first time that day. As for the box, I placed it between my legs, where I could see it all of the time. Cidenet buzzed around me softly, seeming to take in the views, or perhaps he was expectant or even excited. I could not tell. My friend was unreadable.

As I gazed out across the glistening waves, the sun sank in a glorious blaze of colour, painting a wash of reds, purples and pinks across the sky. I listened to the sound of the rippling water, trickling. It was so serene here. Pushing my toes further into the sand, I relished these moments of calm. The last birds were heading off to their nests, preparing to welcome in the night.

"It is time," said Cidenet, appearing in front of me and breaking my serenade with the sea.

I stood and brushed the sand off my feet before pulling on my socks and trainers. Picking up the box, I gazed up at the sky, not sure of what I was expecting. The dragonfly flew to my right shoulder and did the same. By the time I counted to ten, a few dark clouds appeared and began to circle. The sky was still a mixture of reds and pinks, interwoven with purple streaks.

The clouds took on an almost silvery hue and then I gasped as they began to sink, moving down towards the ocean, until they appeared to hover just above it. More wisps sank to the same level, followed by still more, until there was almost a walkway of fluffy, silvery white, stretching across the water and reaching the sand on which I stood. Cidenet flew forward.

Following him, I stepped on to the edge of the cloud, expecting it to give way and my legs to fall through, but it felt solid. My feet sank a little, as though I was walking on a squishy cushion, but I did not slip. Cidenet turned and seemed amused at the expression on my face, which I guessed to be a mixture of exhilaration, marvel and unadulterated fear.

"Don't be afraid," he told me. "You cannot fall, unless you so wish."

"That's reassuring," I said, glancing down at the shimmering water beneath the cloud, which looked as though it were made of silvery wisps, all interwoven, like white candyfloss – it was the closest comparison I could make.

Following Cidenet, my feet sank slightly with every step. When I was a few metres out from the beach, I felt something tremble and vibrate. Nervous, I sat down and tucked my knees in towards my stomach. I had the strangest foreboding of what would happen next. Sure enough, my thoughts came true as the wisp of cloud on which I sat began to slowly ascend.

Cidenet perched on my shoulder. I hugged my knees and peered over the edge. We were still rising and the water sank further away until the reflective shimmers began to blur on the surface. In front of me the purple streaks in the sky grew stronger and darkened, and still we rose.

A lump had formed in my throat, which I put down to sheer fright, but the air around me was breathable. We sailed higher and I imagined this was what it felt like to be a bird flying free, soaring on the arms of the wind, floating and never falling, unless you wanted to.

"It's an amazing view," I remarked, daring myself to look over my shoulder and down at the forest, growing ever smaller.

"It is," Cidenet agreed. "This is my first visit up here."

I was surprised. "Really? How come?"

"I had no reason to," he replied. "And I am not sure how safe it is."

"Now you tell me."

Cidenet's eyes widened and he smiled, before gazing back out to sea. I suspected he had just made a joke.

Something twinkled in the sky and began to enlarge as we approached. It seemed to resemble some kind of floating island, suspended with no visible means of support. Our cloud moved up higher until we were on a level with the strange isle and then it drifted horizontally towards it.

"What is that?" I asked.

"Some call it The Island of the Lost while others call it The Island of the Sacred."

"What do you call it?"

"Alynencia – its old name of legend," replied the dragonfly.

"Is it really an island and how is it floating...?"

"Yes it is and it's magical," was his reply.

Magic? Why, of course.

Chapter 40

I shook my head and watched as our cloud drifted closer to the isle and then stopped, butting against it. The dragonfly flew off my shoulder and ahead of me. Taking that as my cue to get off, I picked up the purple box and stepped on to firm land. As soon as my feet abandoned it, the cloud began to sink.

"How do we get back?" I asked, watching it drift away.

"Same way, I believe..."

"Believe?"

"Yes," answered Cidenet. "I've never been here before."

The light dimmed around us and silver stars flickered in the deep mulberry sky. Surprised it was not black, I wondered why, but colours seemed different here, I reasoned. My feet walked on white sand, which glistened beneath the starlight and seemed to light the way. Trees towered all around, but they were silvery grey. Their leaves shook way above my head, making a whispering sound as I walked, and they were also radiant silver.

"There's a little bunny," I said gleefully, as a fluffy tail bobbed between the trees. "A white one. How cute!"

"The flowers are white too, and silver," remarked Cidenet. "It is a very wondrous world."

"I bet you wish you'd come before."

"If I speak truly, I did not know this place existed. It

is a secret; pure legend. The Only gave me the directions when I asked."

I was surprised. "When did you ask?"

"When the Lady of Nyla told you where the unicorn had last been seen."

I realised then that the dragonfly must communicate with The Only by some kind of telepathy. I wished I knew the skill.

As I walked, I gazed down at the delicate lustrous flower heads that pushed up from the ground. They reminded me of daffodils and daisies, but even more lovely. There was no breeze here and I felt quite warm. No artificial light was necessary as I could see quite well due to the stars reflecting on the silver elements in the sand. On impulse, I bent down and scooped some of it up in my left hand. It felt soft and cool, but not cold. Tiny sparkles lit the sand, and it smelled of the sea and something similar to almonds. Rubbing it between my fingers, I let it slip back to the ground. When it had gone, my skin tingled.

"Which way?" asked the dragonfly. "I have no idea who dwells here, if anyone at all."

I stopped for a second. "I think we should follow this path and see where it takes us. This is such a lovely place to-" I said, but stopped as my legs gave way and I felt myself being thrown upwards into the air.

"Cidenet!" I yelled out in terror as I found myself dangling amongst the branches of the high trees, trapped in a net fashioned out of rope. "Cidenet?" I called again, but in a lower tone. Grabbing the sides of the net, I stabilised my feet in two gaps and raised myself up.

The dragonfly flew close to me immediately, worry

written all over his face. "I will stay out of sight," he said. "Do not panic."

"Don't panic?" I asked. "What's happening? I thought this place was friendly."

"I have never been here before," the insect replied. "I feel responsible as The Only did not warn me. I will try to contact her. I did not know this world was inhabited by humans."

"What can I do?" I asked, glancing down at the ground and experiencing a sharp wave of vertigo. My knees trembled as the grass below seemed to waver.

"You're afraid of heights?"

I nodded. "Always, and I thought that cloud thing was bad enough. So this is another test?" I asked.

"I am only..."

"... the messenger," I concluded. "I know."

The dragonfly smiled wanly and flew into the nearest tree where he concealed himself behind a clump of silvery leaves. I glanced down at the ground and then wished I hadn't as my head whirred. Looking up, I ravaged my thoughts for an idea of what to do.

Remembering the golden bag, I crouched down and moved my legs together, balancing myself against one side of the net, which I gripped tightly with my left hand. Removing the bag from my pocket with the other, I placed it on my lap so that it would not fall. Bracing myself against my twine prison, which I still held on to, I gingerly opened the bag with my fingers that I willed not to tremble.

Inside I saw the familiar blue stone of before, along with a slither of wood, a reddish leaf, a silver orb with the slithery movement of mercury and a feather that reminded me of a peacock's tail. Frowning, I ran my eyes over each one. The right choice was not obvious to me. *Which one will help me?* I had no clue.

As my heart fell, I browsed the trees and listened to the rustling. One mess seemed to follow another, I pondered with a sigh. Carefully replacing each piece in the golden bag, I closed my eyes and shook it gently, before placing my hand back inside. I would take the one that felt right to me.

Running my fingers over the items, I tried to tune in to each one. Concentrating, I noticed they all exuded a different level of warmth, accompanied by a slight vibration. It made me smile. The things were alive, which, I realised, came as no surprise to me. My fingers came to rest upon the rough and rather hot twig, so I removed it. Fastening the bag, I replaced it in my pocket, which I zipped, while keeping the wood in my hand. Glancing around, I noticed Cidenet behind the same leaf as before and it relaxed me.

The box! Oh, no! How had I forgotten?

In panic, I peered downwards and then fell back with a jolt as dizziness and a rising queasiness slid over me. Closing my eyes, I told myself this was only an irrational fear, which my imagination was building up. I would not fall, simply because I couldn't – I was imprisoned in a net. What I was experiencing was vertigo; nothing more and nothing less.

Gripping the twine, I willed myself to gaze down. Trembling, I did so, and the ground shifted before my eyes, rising and falling like the tides. When it cleared, I noticed with dismay that the purple box was lying on the grass immediately below me, in full view of anyone who approached, and there was nothing I could do about it.

Chapter 41

A high-pitch squealing woke me. Getting up, I staggered backwards and slumped against the rope net with my legs sticking up at awkward angles in random holes. In that split second I remembered where I was. I rubbed my head. *How had I managed to fall asleep and how long was I out?*

Glancing down, my breath jammed in my throat as it dawned on me that I was still dreaming. A circle of gigantic white hares with huge hind legs and long, pointed ears were assembled on the glistening, white sand below. Pinching myself, I grimaced as the pain hit. As incredulous as it was, I was not asleep. With revulsion, I spied the jagged teeth of the creatures as they fixed their blood red eyes on me.

"Ci-," I began and then spluttered to a stop. It would not do any good to draw attention to my friend. Biting my tongue, I forced myself to look down. One of the hares had picked up the purple box and was turning it over in his... paws. I shook my head and blinked, but the scene remained unchanged.

Two other hares moved to the tree line where I was suspended and took hold of something that was on the ground. The net with me inside moved. In fright, I realised they were carrying me on the end of a long, wooden pole, which could only mean the strange creatures were extremely strong. I struggled to remain in a crouched position and held on as my rope prison swayed from left to right in perpetual motion. Glancing back to the silver leaves that had concealed the dragonfly, I wondered as to his whereabouts. Is he still hidden there or following me somehow?

The drove of hares carried me through the glittering forest until we reached a place where the trunks were not so closely spaced together. I stopped moving as the long pole came to rest against some trees. Glancing down, I watched the creatures gather together. Muttering sounds that I did not understand in various pitches, they pointed towards a dark ring in the centre of the white sand. I squinted to make out what it was, but I was too high up.

After a while, most of the hares bounced away, a few of them scurrying into the ground. I guessed there were some rather gigantic burrows there. A couple of the menacing looking animals remained beneath me, staring up with bloody eyes. I cringed at their long teeth as they stood guard and hoped they would eventually get bored of me. Glancing around, I tried to fathom an escape route. Where was Cidenet when I needed him? Alas, there was no sign of my little flame-coloured friend.

Hearing a crackle in the air, accompanied by a burning smell, I turned my head and looked down. A sharp intake of breath followed as my stomach lurched. Now I knew what the dark ring in the sand was: the remains of a fire. Now relit, the orangey light glowed against the pale scenery. The true horror of my situation sank in. In some unbelievable irony, I was to be this community's next meal.

Wiping my forehead with the back of my hand, I gazed up at the silver stars flickering in the maroon sky. The place did not seem beautiful anymore. Instead it was eerie, unsettling and dangerous, and I even wished I was back in the witch's cave. That I could handle. Giant hares with jagged teeth were something else.

Sighing, I sat back, rocking the net slightly. Feeling the slither of wood in my hand, I got to thinking. Behind me the trees were close and from my position I could easily step out on to the branches, if only I was not in this net. Thinking fast, I took out the golden bag. As I had already used the blue stone, I presumed, or rather hoped, that I would not require it again. Pulling it out, I threw it with as much force as possible.

Below me, the two hares turned and followed the bluish arc of the glittering pebble, the stars above bouncing off its surface. I imagined it must resemble a shooting star falling from the sky. Quick as a flash, I snapped the slither of wood in two and began to rub the two pieces together, pressing heavily. Within seconds, a spark flew off the surface, followed by a small flame. As I moved it against the side of the net closest to the trees, it began to burn through, not too fast and not too slow. To my relief, the twine did not burst into flames, but gradually disintegrated.

Hearing a squeal from below, I stepped carefully on to the nearest branch while grabbing the bough above me with both hands. Not daring to look down, I walked into the thick mass of silver leaves, carefully balancing along the wooden tightrope on which I found myself. I sensed activity on the ground and imagined all of the hares coming out of their burrows, eager to hunt down their food.

Ignoring anything below, I carried on walking on the branches, hopping from one tree to the next, grasping anything to help me balance. As long as I didn't look to the ground, my vertigo would remain in check and not trouble me. The silvery leaves brushed my face as I continued on my way, rustling in their uncanny way. I wondered if everything here was alive, from talking hares to whispering foliage.

As my wooden path led me further away from the net, I hoped the animals could not climb trees. Bending my head to avoid a swinging bough, a flash of bright red caught my eye. "Cidenet," I gasped.

"You escaped," he remarked. "Well done."

"Ten out of ten for observation," I replied, standing still. "Do you know they were intending to eat me? Cannibal hares!"

"Well, not exactly as you are not a hare."

"You know what I mean, Cidenet, and they're giants. I think I've seen everything now. And I'm not so sure this place is so beautiful anymore."

"We need to get the box," said the dragonfly as he landed on the bough by my head.

My eyes widened. "You're joking?"

Cidenet shook his head and looked extremely serious. "You require it to succeed in your tasks."

"You're not really expecting me to go back?" I asked, and then sighed. "Okay, so you are. What's your plan then because I can't say I have one. Mine was to leg it – and fast!"

"I flew down and checked out the lair of the hares. The leader, who is also the biggest, took the box into his burrow."

I coughed. "You want me to just walk in there and politely ask for it back?"

The insect smiled. "No. I am expecting us to both go down there and take it."

"How?"

"I am only the messenger."

I laughed, unable to stop myself. "You know, that line is becoming most annoying."

Cidenet smirked. "It is not my fault."

Feeling an ache in my shin, I sat down on the branch and rested my back against the mighty trunk. Pulling both legs against my body, I paused to think. The dragonfly swooped down and perched on one of my knees. After a while, I studied him. "Any idea if the hares leave this place?"

Cidenet thought for a moment. "I cannot give you any answers, but I agree it might be a good idea to watch their activities and see if they leave the area, perhaps to hunt?"

I smiled. The creatures probably laid traps in other places and checked them regularly. It was common sense. My friend had given me an idea without actually telling me. "Right," I said, "let's go back and find a place in the trees where we can hide ourselves and see what these evil bunnies are up to, but we'll have to be very quiet."

"I can do quiet very well," replied Cidenet without the slightest buzz.

Chapter 42

Hidden in the safety of the silver leaves, we observed the terrain below as the hares went about their business. They were very talkative, but I did not understand a word. It was probably a good thing, considering the creatures had not been very friendly so far. After about an hour, a group of them headed off in the opposite direction to us, carrying long poles topped with nets. As they stalked off, I hoped they would fail in finding new prey.

A few hares remained seated by the fire, appearing to warm themselves. I wondered how many of them there actually were as it was difficult to count. The exact whereabouts of the leader who had taken the purple box remained a mystery. Although we could see his burrow clearly, I had no idea if he was still inside.

"I'm not sure how long I can wait," I whispered to Cidenet. "I'm getting cramp in my legs. It's hard to sit still and those other hares might come back soon."

The insect nodded.

"We need a distraction," I decided.

I had already thrown the blue pebble, but dare not lose any more items in case I required them for another task. Smiling as a new idea formed in my mind, I removed the remaining half of the slither of wood that did not enflame.

"Cidenet, if I light this, can you fly with it as fast as possible over there and drop it, so all the hares will think there's someone or something in those trees?

Then, if they chase over there, I can try to get to the burrow."

"Are you sure?" he asked.

Nodding, I lit the wood on the trunk of the tree. Before it flickered fully into life, Cidenet scooped it up in his front legs and sped off through the seclusion of the leaves towards the trees yonder. In the distance I spied a flaming object hurtling to the ground. The hares took the bait. As they shot off in the direction of the fire that was now beginning at the base of the tree line, I climbed down.

As soon as I reached the white sand, I ran swiftly towards the fire and the main burrow, which lay behind it. Out of the corner of my eye, I could see the hares battling to put out the fire that threatened their home, imagining they were under attack.

A haze of red jetted past my eyes. It was Cidenet. He blazed a trail in front of me and shot down the man-size burrow before I could reach it. Running behind him down the tunnel, I stopped suddenly as I came face to face with the leader of the hares. A heavy scowl sat between his bloody eyes and his mouth shifted into a loathsome grin. In his grip was Cidenet.

"Put the dragonfly down," I shouted, but the hare only spat a few unintelligible sounds back at me.

The creature was going to crush my friend unless I did something fast. Undoing the bag in my pocket with the fingers of my right hand, I emptied it and pulled it out, hoping to distract him. As the golden material entered the light, it flashed like the burning sun. The hare stepped backwards, his eyes wide and questioning. Uttering something unrecognisable, he stretched a paw towards it. Recognising the look of greed, I expected him to release my friend, but he did not. Time was running out and my reactions were too slow.

Digging my left hand in my pocket, I pulled out the items that remained: the red leaf, the silver orb and the brightly coloured feather. The question was which one. I had to be right and there was no time to waste in deciding. Instinct told me to choose the orb. With shaking fingers, I pushed the leaf and the feather back in my pocket and held up the silvery ball in my hand. The hare did not give it a second glance and advanced on me, staring all the while at the golden bag, which soon slid out of my hand to the ground.

Stepping backwards, I raised the orb higher in the air, wishing for it to do something, anything that might help. I focused so hard on the thing that my fingers unconsciously tightened and I felt it squish under the pressure. As it did so, a blast of fluid fired outwards and hit the hare square in the face. A high-pitched wail filled the burrow as the creature appeared to liquefy, taking on the appearance of mercury. He still resembled a hare, standing there before me with a menacing look on his face, but he could not move. I wondered if he was spellbound.

"Quick!" said Cidenet who was fluttering by my side.

Noticing him for what seemed the first time, my senses flew back to reality and I scooped up the golden bag from the dirt. Shoving it in my pocket, I ran behind the hare into the deeper recesses of the burrow. There the purple box sat. Gathering it up, I raced back, passing what now resembled a harmless silver bunny sculpture. Cidenet took the lead as we exited the tunnel as fast as we could – straight into a hairy ambush.

The circle of hares leered at us and all took a step forward. We were surrounded. I gulped as I took in all of their faces, each one looking angrier than the previous. Glancing at Cidenet, I could see that he was waiting for me to act, so what was stalling me?

I held up the silvery orb in the light of the fire. To my astonishment, the heat seemed to melt it in my grasp and I let go as the fluid spilled on to the sandy ground. I jumped back to avoid it coating my trainers, and as I looked back up, a row of hares as silent as the grave greeted my eyes, each one as still and lifeless as their leader.

"Well done," remarked Cidenet, giving a little buzz.

"Thanks," I replied with a grin. "Shall we be off then, seeing as I'm not going to be bunny supper?"

"I think that would be a good idea," said the insect. "The quicker the better, just in case this spell wears off sooner rather than later."

"Right. Which way?"

"I cannot say. I am only the..."

I shook my head and laughed loudly. "Let's go that way!"

Chapter 43

The silvery trees appeared to move closer together as I walked. Edging to the side, I tried to move around them, but they shifted in front of me. I noticed the sand rippling - what was happening? Cidenet looked at me and glanced away, apparently unnerved by the same things that worried me. Tightening my grip on the purple box in my hand, I decided to outwit the trees. Dashing to the right, I ran as fast as I could, but they seemed to know and echoed my movements, shutting me out.

"I give up," I announced, as the whispering of the leaves seemed to grow louder.

Cidenet crept on to my shoulder, and I guessed he had just read my thoughts and knew what I was about to do. Quick as a flash, I darted to the left and the right, and back again, tracing zigzag patterns, which the trees could not match, and then I took a big leap forward as the trunks shifted. I was through.

We were in a round clearing. As the boughs creaked and the leaves whispered behind me, I saw him materialise before my eyes, his white hide coated with a resplendent silver sheen. He studied me with piercing black eyes. Dipping his single horn, he trod the ground with his front hooves. I stood transfixed, unable to move. I was looking at the last unicorn.

With a side glance at Cidenet, who fluttered down from my shoulder to my side, I stepped forward slowly. The mystical creature before me did not move, but observed me, as though curious. I took another hesitant step, followed by one more, and then paused, but not out of choice. In front of me there seemed to be a kind of barrier. Looking down, I noticed a silver line on the ground, tracing a circle all around the unicorn. I wondered if it was a protective shield of some kind, designed to ward off enemies. Glancing up at the creature, he seemed unafraid and trod the ground in an indifferent motion, his tail swishing idly behind him.

Reaching up with my left hand, I touched the air in front of me. My fingers tingled as I felt something solid, but invisible. Unsure of what to do, I surveyed the vicinity. The trees seemed to nod knowingly and the whispering died down to an unnerving silence. In my right hand, the small box grew warm. Raising it to my waist, I cradled it in both palms, examining it. I seemed to feel the object inside. Looking up, I noticed the unicorn move his head to one side, focusing on me with renewed interest. I wondered if he knew what I had brought him.

In my hands the purple box began to glow, soft and warm. Glancing at the creature before me, I raised the precious gift slowly, aiming for him to see it more clearly. To my astonishment he swished his tail and reared his head, his beautiful silvery mane flowing in the slight breeze, and then he walked towards me, holding his head high, so tall and majestic.

Time stood still. My breath caught in my throat as he approached, his silvery hide glinting. Looking down, I noticed his hooves were also silver. The dark eyes were hypnotic as they stared straight at me, through me, as if the beast was trying to communicate something. Upon reaching an arm's distance away, he raised his head and snorted. The invisible shield still separated us.

The unicorn gazed down at the square box in my hands and narrowed his eyes. Then he reared up on his hind legs and threw his head back. Afraid, I staggered backwards a couple of steps, but remembering the protective shield between us, I halted. The creature could not reach me, I realised, standing my ground. The whispering of the leaves began again in the once eerie silence. Cidenet was quiet. I could not discern the faintest buzz from his wings.

Pressing my feet hard against the ground to keep my balance, I stared up at the unicorn, unable to read his expression. Then I heard someone ask me, "What is it you carry?" Glancing around, I spied no one and then realised the deep voice was inside my head. I gazed up at the creature that was now standing once more on his four powerful legs. Oddly, his eyes appeared to soften.

Frightened, but trying to keep my wits about me, I replied slowly, "The Lady of Nyla asked me to bring this to you. It was guarded by a witch in a cave in the forest."

"What lies within?"

"She told me it was the heart of the unicorn and that I must return it to you."

With a shake of his silvery mane, the majestic creature stepped through the shimmering, casting the purest light all around me, and I took a step back.

"There is no need to fear me," said the voice, and I stopped moving. "Please open the box, if you will. I have waited an eternity for my heart's return."

With shaking fingers I turned the golden key in the golden lock until there sounded a dull click. Glancing up, I noticed the unicorn looking down at my fingers, searchingly. His mane was resplendent, resembling a trickle of stars, and his beautiful eyes shone. I realised in that moment that I had nothing to fear from him. Instead, I had the soothing feeling that I was safe, that he would protect me from any danger.

The buzzing of Cidenet's wings met my ears above the whispering of the leaves and I wondered why I had not been able to hear them before. Gripping the box tightly with my left hand, I opened the lid with the other. Shots of sterling light fired out, blinding me for a second, and I felt the box shake. Gripping it with both hands, I held on as the vibration travelled up my arms and into my shoulders.

Struggling to stand, I tried to focus, but it was nigh impossible, conscious as I was of nothing but this dazzling blaze of light. Within seconds I was sitting on the ground, but I had managed to hold on to the box somehow. At the point where I thought I could take it no more, the glow vanished and I could see the clearing again.

The unicorn was still there, gazing down at me, but now he had a companion. Cidenet perched on my knee as I gazed up at the two mythical beasts, standing still, their long necks entwined, magical in their silvery whiteness. I blinked. *There are two of them?* I thought of the words of the Lady of Nyla and realised the heart had actually been the creature's long-lost mate. I smiled. There was no longer only one, but two, so perhaps the species would not die out. Now there was a hope it would survive.

"I'm glad you're not the last," I said finally.

The spell that had been worked between the two creatures broke and they pulled away from one another.

The larger male turned towards me, his dark eyes glowing. "You have my eternal gratitude," he told me. "You cannot know how long I have waited. I had given up on ever seeing my heart again. To return it must have cost you."

"It didn't cost me anything," I replied, standing up. "And Cidenet helped me."

"You must have had to overcome many fears."

I nodded. "Yes, but I'm happy you're no longer alone."

The female unicorn stepped forward. "You have my utmost gratitude also." I heard her words in my mind, her voice rippling like a waterfall. "I was separated from him by a spell that bound me in that box. I thought I would never return here. Now my own heart is full."

"Do you have a task for me?" I asked, smiling. "I have one more left to do."

These wondrous beasts looked at one another and back at me. "I do not," replied the female, looking at her mate. He nodded to her before turning to me. "I must seek the advice of The Only," he answered, digging his hooves into the ground.

Cidenet fluttered upwards as a shower of sweet-smelling yellow flowers floated down around us, coating everything in sight. I held out my palms as they filled with petals. Before my eyes the glorious butterfly shimmered into existence, swept in on the silent breeze. I took in the golden wings with the dazzling orange tips, the ebony body and the deep crimson eyes.

"I bid you good day," she said, setting a warm smile upon me. "You have done well, Jayne. You fearlessly faced your tasks and returned the heart of the unicorn to its rightful place."

"Thanks," I replied, blushing. "But I only did four tasks."

The Only nodded. "The final, fifth task, will take you to the place you seek, the end of your journey. Do you still wish it?"

Clasping my hand over my mouth in a bid to contain my emotion, I nodded as I glanced sideways at Cidenet. "I do. I do so wish it."

"Then it shall be," The Only replied. "The unicorn will be your guide."

I looked to the majestic creature, standing tall and silent, curious to know what my next challenge would be, and which fear I would need to overcome this time. "Thank you," I said, bowing to the giant butterfly. "Thank you for helping me."

"My only wish was for you to realise your true destiny," she answered. "My part is done. I bid you farewell."

Golden petals filled the air until nothing stirred where the butterfly once stood.

Chapter 44

"What is my final task?" I asked Cidenet.

The male unicorn stepped forward and bowed his head. "I must ask you if you dare."

I shrugged. "To do what?"

"Dare to ride with me," the unicorn answered mysteriously.

I glanced at the dragonfly, whose wings were still, but he had no words to give me.

"Your task is to hold on," explained the unicorn. "I will need to travel through time itself to take you to the place you seek. You will need to keep up with me."

"What if I cannot?"

The unicorn shook his head, ignoring my question. "Are you ready?"

"I-I don't k-know," I mumbled, experiencing a sudden dread of the unknown and sadness that I must leave.

I looked at Cidenet, my faithful protector and guide, who rose now to flutter softly in the air. As I wondered whether he was reading my thoughts, he nodded with a wistful smile.

"Cidenet!" I exclaimed. "How can I leave you? Can you come with me?"

The dragonfly's red colours faded for a second and he shook his head solemnly. "I am afraid not," he replied. "I must remain here in this world, but I will always think of you."

Tears sprung to my eyes as he spoke and I blinked them back. "I will always remember you, too," I told him, holding out my hand so that he would land on it. "You have been a good friend to me. I will never forget. I wish you could come with me, but I understand. I wish you lots of happy things!"

Cidenet grinned broadly. "And I wish you happiness also. I hope you will be reunited with the one your heart longs for. It has been a pleasure to serve you."

"You are a true friend, Cidenet."

"We must leave," announced the unicorn, breaking the moment. "I fear the space in time for our leaving is short. Do you dare to ride with me?"

"I dare," I replied, and the dragonfly flittered a small distance away from my hand. "Goodbye," he said.

I returned his wistful smile. "Goodbye."

Stepping towards the great unicorn with a mixture of fear, trepidation and excitement, I pondered what might happen next. *Will I reach Entyre? If not, where?* I tried to put the thoughts out of my head as my heart raced. Leaving Cidenet was gut-wrenching and I was surprised at how much I would miss him, but I sensed that time was running out and I had to move quickly.

The silvery beast crouched down so that I could clamber on to his back. "Hold on to my reins," he said when I was seated.

"What reins?" I began and then noticed two thin, but strong threads appear in my hands. I nodded as the great creature stood up. I was far from the ground.

"Goodbye, my friend," I called out to Cidenet, who nodded and buzzed loudly. He did not reply. I wondered if he did not wish to say the words again because they sounded too final.

Next I turned to look at the female unicorn, who blinked and smiled warmly at me. She tossed her mane and neighed, to which the male responded with the same. I realised fondly that they were inseparable and wondered how old they were. *Do mythical creatures live forever?* I turned my head to ask, but the world seemed to shake and all of the trees faded to nothing. The clearing was no more and stars twinkled all around me. The sky had turned dark and we were moving.

Chapter 45

Glancing down to my side, I saw the powerful legs of the unicorn galloping in the night, but there was no ground below us. It was as if we were advancing through the air, suspended by some powerful force. The stars rushed by, accompanied by delicate wisps of white cloud. I gripped the silver cords in my hands and focused forward, willing my body to balance as the mighty creature gathered speed and the wind swept through my fiery hair.

It was cold, but we were travelling fast; through space and time, I guessed. The acceleration made my heart race and my skin felt as though it were covered with goose bumps. For some reason I found myself laughing; in amazement, wonder or fear, I did not know. I supposed it was a mixture of all three. I missed the bright dragonfly already. If only he could have accompanied me. I pondered what he would have thought of the city beneath the sea and then hoped I would reach it. *What if I do not?* I cast the thought from my mind immediately.

"Hold on," said a voice in my head, ripping through my imaginings.

We sailed down through the sky, past the glittering stars that twinkled in the pitch black. The unicorn seemed to be falling, but as I peered down over his haunches, I could see his hooves moving in a soundless rhythm. He was galloping fast as we travelled down through the heavens in an endless plummet. I held on tightly as my hair whisked upwards above my head in spirals. Somehow I stayed on the unicorn's back, but I have no idea how as we were falling rapidly.

"Is this time? Are we passing through time?" I asked, my voice trembling.

"Yes, all the times long past. Do not let go of the reins," the voice instructed, "whatever happens."

I shivered as his words. *What will happen?* I cast out the thought and gritted my teeth as I gripped the silvery strands ever more tightly. *How long will we fall?*

I looked to the right and left, but only saw endless impenetrable darkness, filled with random sparkles. That was all. Then wisps of colourful light whizzed past me. Reds, greens, blues filled the sky, creating a rainbow against the dark, littered with stars. I blinked as the hues grew brighter and I steadied myself.

The unicorn halted his plunge. We were galloping straight again, seemingly supported by solid ground, but there was nothing there. I stopped trying to rationalise everything and steadied myself, wondering how far the distance would be. A million colourful strobes of light shot past us as the unicorn travelled ever faster. Whether we were riding through space or time, I could not be sure. I held my breath.

Chapter 46

A faint glimmer shone ahead in the darkness and we plummeted out of the sky towards the ground. The unicorn kept his movements steady and seemed to canter through the air, so I remained on his back as steady as ever. My hair whirled around my face, tickling my chin, but I ignored it, gripping the silver reins in my hands as tightly as I could. In some unfathomable way I did not want the ride to end, as fantastic as it was, but I yearned to reach my destination.

I do not know how long or how far we fell in this never-ending vertical ride, but eventually we landed on a beach, long and wide. The violent roar of the sea was deafening. Swishing his mane and bringing himself to a careful stop, the unicorn turned his mighty head to look at me.

"You did well," I heard him say between my own imaginings. "You held on."

I nodded, feeling half out of breath and half dizzy from the excitement of the ride. "I think you helped me to keep my balance."

The sturdy beast blinked his dark eyes. "I did nothing. You kept your own."

I smiled, not knowing what to say.

The unicorn stared out across the dark sea. "Do you not recognise where we are?"

Shaking my head, I followed the direction of his eyes. It was night, but I could not guess the time, and there was a chill in the air. The strong wind churned the waters, which raged, tossing up endless streams of surf. From above, the moon gazed down upon the waves.

"I have no idea," I admitted. "Where are we?"

"We rode through time and space to reach this place. You should recognise it as you have been here before."

Looking around, I frowned and made to dismount, but a word of warning sounded in my ears. "Stay on my back. Danger lurks in these sands."

Danger? My imagination surged forth, sweeping through a wave of memories. "This is the same beach?" I exclaimed, bewildered. "So you did bring me back, not to the city beneath the sea, but to the beach. Thank you!" Reaching forwards against the harsh wind, I hugged the unicorn's neck with both of my arms. He felt warm and his silver-dusted hide glistened in the moonlight, reminding me that this was not a horse! "Sorry," I mumbled, sitting back up. "I didn't mean to grab you like that."

I heard a rush of laughter in my mind; a rippling of light was how it sounded. The unicorn turned his head to look at me once more. "I am still a creature who appreciates gratitude," he replied. "But there is something I must tell you."

I sat still with the reins lying loose in my lap, scared of what he might say.

"I have brought you back to where you wanted to go. This is your heart's desire?"

Taking a deep breath, I replied, "Yes."

"You have returned, but it was not in my power to take you back to the point in time when you left. You probably remember the peril that lurks in these sands. I sense your fear, so we will wait."

"For what?" I asked. "I don't understand. What do you mean by this not being the same place in time?"

The silver creature swished his mane. "We have returned to an earlier time. I could only fix on the earliest point that you first arrived here... before. So, we are here, but you have not been to the city of Entyre yet. You will not have met..."

Realising what he meant, I felt tears course down my cheeks. Wiping them with the back of my hand, I struggled with my feelings and my fear. What had I done? I had thrown my old life away on a romantic whim and not even succeeded in that. I bit down hard on my lip to lessen the pain I felt in my chest.

"Do not fear," said the voice. "You did succeed. The same things that happened that day will occur again."

"But I've changed since then. I've learned so much. I'm not the same."

"So you have. You will return as you are now, unchanged, in common with your destiny, but the timeline has altered. In a short while I will ask you to step down on to the sand."

"But there are invisible things... they tried to kill me," I protested as fear surged up my spine.

"I will be here," the creature assured me. "Nothing will happen to you. I am here to protect you. But you must be brave. You must lie on the sand, as you did long ago, and wait. You must repeat your actions of yesterday. The strands of time must connect. You will have to endure the fear again, but you will once more be united with your heart, as you reunited me with mine."

Taking a deep breath, I steadied myself and twisted my hair back into a rough knot. I had to trust him; he had brought me this far, and I knew he would indeed protect me. There was no reason for him to act falsely. I nodded and the dark eyes of the unicorn met mine. I felt certain he smiled somehow and a sudden warmth fell over me. In that moment I had no fear; there was nothing to be anxious of. Soon I would meet my love again, but I just had to endure one last thing. Perhaps this was the final task: to have faith in my protector.

"I trust you," I replied. "I will do as you say. Thank you for bringing me back. I owe you so much. What can I do to repay you?"

"You already did it," the unicorn's words echoed in my mind. "I wish you everything your heart desires."

Realising that I could not say goodbye again today, I swung myself down from the great creature's back and landed softly on the damp sand. I stroked the silvery white hide for the last time and held back my tears. So this was the end of my adventure so far and a new door beckoned, but it was also an old one. I would be returning, but it would be a re-beginning. Everything would be repeated, but it would be different this time.

I had my memories and all the things I had learned during my journey. Perhaps I would repeat some mistakes, but I might sense which to avoid. With new realisation, I reached into my pocket and pulled out the crystal that I had carried all this time. No longer did I need it, and I refused to let its power endanger my future again. I knew what I wanted. With no more hesitation, I raised my arm and threw the crystal into the sea to be lost on the waves. It sank into the darkness.

Chapter 47

The unicorn trotted softly away and I stood motionless, battling my anxiety. The cold night wrapped its icy fingers around me and the wailing wind tore at my hair as I waited in silence. As before, a year ago, the ground beneath me gave way and I fell on the damp ground. I breathed heavily and spat out sand, while my fear set my heart pounding against my ribs. Coughing, I struggled to stand, but I found that I could not move my legs.

In the silence the desolate wails began to sound from the depths of the sea, becoming gradually higher in pitch. I covered my head with my hands as the ear-splitting noise swallowed the air. Closing my eyes, I waited for the end, but then I remembered. Looking up, I saw the unicorn standing still and watching. His dark eyes bore a soft expression. "Have no fear," he told me. "I will not leave."

A faint smile brushed my lips and I knew I could endure anything. This had happened before, but this time it was different. I gazed at my protector and focused on him. The biting wind blew harder, but I did not shift my eyes away from the silvery creature glowing like a light in the darkness. In the distance the wailing heightened as if the sea itself were crying. Icy fingers flickered through my hair and around my throat. Taken aback, I screamed, but it was more out of instinct than fear. I knew deep inside that there was nothing to be scared of this time. He would come.

The unicorn did not stray. I sensed he would not leave until I did. Still, I yelled louder until I felt my lungs would burst as the icy hands covered my face. Kicking my feet, I fought my attacker, but I could neither feel nor see it. The invisible thing tightened its grip around my neck. "Have no fear," spoke the unicorn in my mind. "I will be here."

Coughing, I struggled not to lose consciousness. In the dark I saw a familiar face with eyes as dark as the sea and hair as blue as its deepest depths. "Come into the waves," he said, the words piercing the silence. It was not the unicorn who spoke, but him. He was here, although he did not know me yet. My heart seemed to rush into my throat and I fought the urge to laugh or cry; I did not know which emotion was the stronger, but my fear was subsiding. I tried to move my head, but the cold hands pushed it flat against the wet sand. Tasting salt in my mouth, I dug my hands into the sand and hauled my body forwards using all of my strength.

"Come into the waves," repeated the voice, its tremors sailing softly upon the lapping water, now inches away from my face.

"Have no fear," said the unicorn and I smiled at him one last time before I finally dragged my aching body into the waiting waves.

As I floated, unafraid, I looked back to shore to bid him goodbye. In the dim distance I thought I saw two figures. They moved out of the tree line and stood still. One raised an arm and pointed towards the ocean, towards me. I trod water, squinting in the darkness. "How can it be?" I gasped as realisation hit me. I moved nearer to the shore and stood up in the shallow waves, not daring to step on the sand.

Chapter 48

"Jayne!"

The name echoed across the beach, closing the distance, as tears of joy sprung to my eyes. I saw him step forward, but then the other figure in the shadows held him back, wisely. It was her. My stomach jolted and my unsaid words stuck solid in my throat. I glanced at the unicorn, my protector, who was still there, but looking at me with an unreadable expression. *My protector, but could he be theirs, too..?*

The mighty creature flung back his silvery mane and turned around. My heart sank. He was leaving. How would they cross the beach? It was too dangerous. I would have to help them.

With my mind racing, I stepped forward, but in that split second the unicorn turned. I froze under his gaze. Then I knew; he was answering me. Within seconds he had galloped as far as the dark tree line. I covered my mouth with my hand, trembling in the happiness that threatened to overwhelm me. I coughed and half laughed as I wiped away the tears that now streamed down my face.

The unicorn appeared before me, his hooves cutting through the waves, and I could contain my excitement no longer. Standing on tiptoe, I wound my arms around his neck and kissed his warm, bristly head as my grandfather and Sophia dismounted. "Thank you," I whispered.

"Jayne," mumbled my grandfather, grasping me to him as if he had not seen me in years. Glancing at his face, I knew it to be true, for he had aged. Then I looked at Sophia, who in contrast looked decades younger and wore the most wondrous smile.

"How?" I asked, dumbfounded, as the waters swarmed around us.

Sophia nudged my grandfather, who smiled. "It was his idea," she explained. "We waited... a while. It has been nearly ten years and then he contracted cancer, incurable. It was your note that brought us together. When you died, he visited me."

"Died?" I gasped, and then I saw an image of myself throwing the crystal into the ocean. Understanding, I nodded. "Time is strange. I've only been gone a week, but it seems so much longer."

Sophia smiled, not comprehending. "I told him my story and he believed me; the first person who ever did. He wanted to find you, and I warned him what happened to me, but he was stubborn. He checked the exact date and time that you sank into the first coma, and he promised that we would find you on that very day at that very time. I was afraid, and so we waited until the time came that we could not wait."

"The cancer," I said, staring into my grandfather's soft eyes.

Sophia nodded silently.

"It was because of you that we met," continued my grandfather. "That note you left, it haunted me. When you fell into a coma again, I was devastated. The doctors said the virus had remained in your system and weakened it, but your letter kept me going. I treasured it, kept rereading it, and hoped you would wake up. When you died suddenly, it was too much. I needed answers, and so I visited Sophia. She showed me a photograph from Entyre, but it was not like our photos. It was like ice. And then I saw her paintings and I realised the story you told me was true."

"I'm so happy," I replied, wiping the tears from my eyes. "I missed you so much. It was selfish of me to go."

My grandfather shook his head. "No, Jayne, I thought about this a lot and I'd probably have done the same thing. The temptation would have been too great. I think you get your sense of adventure from me. Normal is not enough."

I laughed and hugged him again, but time, it seemed, was growing impatient. A sudden crash of the darkening waves brought me back to reality and reminded me of the danger we were still in. Fearful, I looked behind me, on to the beach, but he was still there, the unicorn, as constant as the wailing wind.

"I think we should go," suggested Sophia.

"Where?" asked my grandfather.

I turned to stare in the direction of the horizon. "There, where you can see a man in the sea. There's nothing to be scared of. I've been here before. The man is someone I want you to meet, but from the moment I see him it will be as if I've never been to Entyre. The unicorn told me. I will forget everything that happened there in the past, but not my journey back here since. Time will flex and start again."

"Are you afraid?" asked my grandfather, taking my hand.

I looked into his eyes and shook my head. "Not anymore."

After watching my companions wander deeper into the water, I took a deep breath and turned my head to look at the unicorn once more. Blinking his piercing black eyes, he raised his head and neighed against the roar of the sea, and in that moment I knew that I would never see him again. As I stepped backwards into the cold swell, he lingered there on the sand, steadfast until the end, protecting. As I had brought him his heart, so he had returned mine. I no longer felt the ache of guilt or loss, or loneliness. With joy consuming me, I swam strongly towards my destiny, feeling confident in the water with which I now felt as one.

The End
To be continued

Thank you for buying this book. I hope you enjoyed it. Please leave a review – feedback is always welcome and I'd love to know what you thought of the story, Vickie Johnstone.

Author links

Kiwi Series website: www.kiwiincatcity.com
Twitter: @vickiejohnstone
Blog: www.vickiejohnstone.blogspot.com
Goodreads: www.goodreads.com/author/show/4788773.Vickie_Johnstone
Facebook: www.facebook.com/AuthorVickieJohnstone
Gift Shop: www.zazzle.co.uk/kiwiincatcity

About the author's other books

The Kiwi Series (for readers aged 10 up, teens & adults)

Have you ever wished your cat could talk or wondered where he/she goes when you are not around? *Kiwi in Cat City* is the first book in a series, of which there are six fun adventures. Kiwi seems like a typical moggie, content to nap in the sun and chase shadows, but she has a secret. She is a magical cat from a place called Cat City. With her two humans, James and Amy, Kiwi finds mysteries and adventures, dealing with catnappings, jewel thieves, giant mice, time travel, haunted houses, Father Christmas, pyramids and more. The fun stories contain positive messages about loyalty, friendship, honesty, bullying and the power of standing together.

~ *Kiwi in Cat City (book 1)*

One dark night, Amy cannot sleep and she looks out of the window into the garden to see her cat, Kiwi, transfixed by the moon, which is glowing brightly like a cat's claw. Waking her brother, James, Amy suggests they follow Kiwi to see where she goes... whether it involves a hunt for mice or something else. Little do they know that, with a flick of her tail, Kiwi is going to magically change them into kittens and lead them on the adventure of their lives to a land they never knew existed in their wildest dreams. In the blue-lit world of Cat City, the budding detectives help Inspector Furrball to solve the mystery of the missing catizens and find out what happened to Madame Purrfect.

- Kiwi and the Missing Magic (book 2)

James and Amy embark on their second adventure with their black cat, which will take them to the Land of Giant Mice in search of the missing Magic. They return to Cat City to help their friends and meet some new characters along the way, including the Worry Bee, Whiskers and Moggie. Can James and Amy help Kiwi save the day? More importantly, will James' pet hamster find his true calling in life?

- Kiwi and the Living Nightmare (book 3)

Amy, James and Kiwi embark on their spookiest adventure yet - on Halloween. What begins with an eerie dream about a three-legged cat will take the budding detectives on a quest to find an old house in the middle of the woods, meeting some familiar characters and some perky squirrels along the way. Little do they know that there awaits an angry, restless ghost that will do anything to stop them leaving. Meanwhile, Furrball and Siam discover the human world, and some surprising news.

- Kiwi and the Serpent of the Isle (book 4)
Finalist in the Indie Excellence Book Awards 2013

The wedding of Inspector Furrball and Madame Purrfect approaches, but, catastrophe, the ring is stolen from the Gem Shop! A pawprint identifies Fyre Cracker as the thief, but he lives in the dark world of the UnderPaw beneath Cat City, which is inhabited by crimicats. It's up to the Kiwi Klub to find the ring. In the human world, the hamsters decide to stand up for their rights to better plastic wheels and an abundance of sunflower seeds. Meanwhile, the dastardly Dev shocks Kiwi with the news that he knows a big secret about her family – that her father, Delphinius, may still be alive! The key is The Sculptor, who will lead Kiwi and friends on their biggest adventure yet – to the strange Isle of the Serpent where they will come face to face with their most dangerous adversary so far.

~ *Kiwi in the Realm of Ra (book 5)*

Inspired by the film *Back to the Future*, Whiskers invents The Time-Squeaking Mouse. He plans to take his friends on a fantastic trip to celebrate Amy's thirteenth birthday. However, the time machine falls into the wrong hands and dastardly Dev travels back to Ancient Egypt when cats were sacred. With Dev having changed the path of history, it's up to Kiwi and the gang to travel back in time to find him. What will Kiwi, Amy, James, Whiskers, Hammy, Misty, Furrball and Siam think of this desert world of tombs, pyramids and sacred gods?

~ *Kiwi's Christmas Tail (book 6)*

Amy, James and Kiwi find a star. But this is no ordinary star. He's living and breathing, and his name is Sharissimo. A year earlier, the star and a fairy called Lilabel were captured by an evil witch with a big wart on her nose. While Sharissimo managed to escape, Lilabel could not. Can Amy, James and Kiwi find the fairy before Christmas Eve and rescue her from the clutches of the witch? The witch herself is in for a shock when she finds herself in the furry land of Cat City.

~ Day of the Living Pizza
(book 1 in the Smarts & Dewdrop Mystery series)
(comedy/detective/horror for kids & adults)

Detective Smarts of Crazy Name Town has a problem. Doctor Boring and his receptionist have been bumped off, and the only clues at the scene are some olives, tomatoes, mushrooms and sprinkles of oregano. With the town folk dropping like flies and strange figures stumbling down the streets, Officer Dewdrop has an idea.

~ Day of the Pesky Shadow (book 2)

Detective Smarts is still finding it hard to look at a pizza, never mind eat one. But there is a new mind-boggler to solve - who is the mysterious, dark figure causing the townsfolk's legs to go wibbly wobbly? Smarts and sidekick Dewdrop are hot on the trail.

~ 3 Heads and a Tail
(comedy/romance/fantasy for over 16s)

When nature lover Josie moves into a house share with two pals, dreamer Ben and model man David, she sees it as a short stop and doesn't bank on an attraction developing with one of them. Meanwhile, Ben's dog, Glen, has the hots for Miss Posh, the beautiful golden Lab in the park. When dog meets dog it's puppy love, but a complication leads to Glen taking matters into his own paws. In this comedy of errors, romance and walkies, it's anyone's guess who is going to get the girl/dog and live happily ever after. Written for the NaNoWriMo 2011 competition.

~ I Dream of Zombies (book 1)
(horror for adults)

A zombie novel set in London over six weeks in 2013. It all begins on a summer's day with the media reporting with some hilarity that people are dreaming of the dead coming to life, but those who have dreamt them are convinced they are a warning of things to come. All over London there are incidences of people becoming sick and aggressive. As the attacks mount, the media is forced to take the matter seriously. Marla, Ellen and Tommy find themselves fighting for their survival as their sense of reality is smashed. Will the army and police maintain control or will the UK find itself in lock down, isolated from the outside world?

~ Haven (book 2)

Marla, Ellen and Tommy escape to a government facility that has become a refuge for civilians.

~ Kaleidoscope

119 poems, divided under themes: love; creatures; nature; dark side; abstracts; figures and childhood.

~ Travelling Light

A free book of 38 poems.

~ Life's Rhythms

316 haiku on various subjects and themes.

Printed in Great Britain
by Amazon